HOPE SURVIVES

AFTER THE EMP BOOK NINE

HARLEY TATE

HOPE SURVIVES

A POST-APOCALYPTIC SURVIVAL THRILLER

If danger shows up uninvited, how far would you go to keep your family safe?

In the middle of a brutal Northern California winter, Walter Sloane cranks up a homemade radio anticipating nothing but static. When a commanding voice proclaims a new America is rising, Walter rushes to tell the others. He doesn't know a much bigger problem is already at his door.

Can a new alliance survive the ultimate test?

Tracy Sloane is winding down a twenty-four hour shift guarding a pharmacy in the middle of town. When two strangers show up ready for battle, she barely makes it out alive. If she can't convince the Jacobsons to do what's right, their new alliance might be dead on arrival —literally.

The end of the world brings out the best and worst in all of us.

Faced with the prospect of war with a neighboring group and the threat of military intervention from afar, the Sloanes find themselves between a rock and a hard place. They'll have to fight for their survival, their future, and their way of life. Every decision might be their last.

The EMP is only the beginning.

Hope Survives is book nine in the *After the EMP* series, a post-apocalyptic thriller series following ordinary people trying to survive after a geomagnetic storm destroys the nation's power grid.

Subscribe to Harley's newsletter and receive an exclusive companion short story, *Darkness Falls*, absolutely free.
www.harleytate.com/subscribe

300 DAYS WITHOUT POWER

CHAPTER ONE

SILAS

Donner Summit Bridge
    Outside Truckee, California
    9:00 a.m.

Silas pulled into the empty observation point and killed the engine. The snow-covered roads were no match for the snowmobile, even with abandoned cars and looted tractor-trailers stalled out along Donner Pass. He reached into his pack and fished out his binoculars.

Donner Lake stretched in an east/west line below him and thanks to a steady wind at his back, the usual morning fog and clouds were nonexistent. He scanned the coastline with his naked eyes first, searching for the telltale rise of smoke from a chimney or the unexpected movement of a person against the snow.

Nothing.

He did the same with his binoculars, glassing the

waterline and up into the mountains, coming to rest on the property the Cunningham clan now called home. Once Donner Lake Motor Court, the resort on the water had become so much more over the past nine months.

Gone were the tourists and the people incapable of surviving in this new world. In their place were enterprising compatriots bound together in a singular mission: to stay alive and rebuild by whatever means necessary.

Elias Cunningham, the leader of their group, had a singular vision. It had taken Silas a while to come to terms with his uncle's radical approach, but after more than one run-in with looters and thieves who would kill as soon as trade, Silas saw the point.

Ensuring the family's survival required more than just a small resort on the edge of a lake. Long-term living took resources only a town could provide. He exhaled and lowered the binoculars.

Donner Lake had been good to them up until now. Only two ways in, both secured by round-the-clock shifts of watchers. Plenty of coastline to fish. A lodge big enough to house most of their family with peripheral cabins close enough for the rest.

In the beginning, they had welcomed all comers. Most of their immediate family subscribed to the "shit happens" outlook on life, rallying together the second the grid collapsed. A few who hoped some ninny from the government would come save them held out for the first week or two. By then, Elias had already cleared the resort by whatever means necessary.

Silas spat in the snow as memories dragged bile up his throat. The hard part hadn't lasted long. At the peak, their ranks swelled to fifty-five, all blood or marriage relations apart from Donnie's girlfriend Maria who came with her own arsenal of AR-15s and a trunk full of ammo. Elias let her stay even without a wedding ring. But it had been a rough fall and winter. Deals were made that shouldn't have been. Accidents happened and supplies were lost. Good people died.

Their ranks had shrunk to forty-three and Silas lost the only person who gave a damn about him since he was a kid: his father. Butch Cunningham had gone on a gun run and never come home. Neither had the arsenal of weapons he'd promised to deliver. Not knowing what happened to the man twisted Silas up for months, but the cold weather snapped him out of it.

He couldn't putter around Donner Lake with idle hands and plenty of liquor. Elias was right; dominating the lake wasn't sufficient. With two feet of snow on the ground, raids became dangerous and less frequent. Hunting became sporadic and fishing almost impossible.

Too many guys like Silas forced to sit around and wait while the temperatures hovered around freezing. With Elias's vision, they would never be lazy again. A new town would rise out of the smoldering ashes of Truckee. One that would withstand anything nature or man could throw at it.

A modern-day fortress for the Cunninghams to own.

An engine rumbled in the distance and Silas turned, one hand resting on the rifle strap across his chest. A snowmobile rounded the curve and whipped into the observation area, parking alongside Silas with a flourish of ice flecks.

Beckett pulled off his helmet and the breeze blew his bushy red hair into his eyes. "There better be a damn good reason for scouting in this wretched wind."

Silas unlatched his saddlebag and pulled out a map. It crinkled as it unfolded and he cursed. Beckett was right to be annoyed; the frigid morning air made everything from taking a piss to reading contour lines a thousand times harder. "You know Elias is sick of waiting. He wanted us out here last week."

He tugged off a glove with his teeth and shoved it in his pocket before working the kinks out of the worn paper. Elias would box his ears if he ripped a single corner. Maps were worth more than gold. "Help me hold this."

Beckett reached for the left edge and pulled the map taut.

Blowing a lungful of warm air over his fingers, Silas warmed them enough to trace the ridge of the foothills around the town. He pointed at the Summit Bridge. "We're here. The main part of Truckee sits at a low point past the lake."

"Tell me something I don't know."

Silas cut Beckett a glance, but continued. "The Truckee River snakes alongside Interstate 80 and splits the town in two. South of the highway, the elevations dip into the five thousands."

"That's good, right? Lower means water and maybe some flat parts for farming."

"It's not that easy. It's the oldest part of town and full of brick warehouses and abandoned mills. When I canvassed it in the fall, I barely made it out alive. It's full of people."

"Even now?"

Silas glanced up at the lake in the distance. "If they aren't all dead and frozen, then, yeah. Truckee's population was right about sixteen thousand. Elias says ninety percent should be dead by now, but that leaves what? Over fifteen hundred people still out there, hanging on."

"But they can't all be in that one area."

"We'd have to clear it building by building." Silas exhaled. "With the sheer number of abandoned warehouses, we would never be able to eliminate all the threats."

"Then where?" Beckett turned back to the map. "Elias said somewhere with infrastructure and buildings we could secure."

Silas pointed out the northwest quadrant of town. Perched above the lake, the area hovered right around seven thousand feet. "I'm thinking this area."

"But that's just resorts and ski lodges."

"That means they should be empty."

"But how's that any better than what we have now?" Beckett shook his head. "Elias wants a city. Not more log cabins in the snow."

"Look closer." Silas pointed out two roads. "There

are only two ways in to the whole area. We already control Donner Pass and the cutoff north of Donner Lake Motor Court. That only leaves Northwoods Boulevard."

Beckett snorted. "So what?"

"What's on the north side of I-80 at the exit ramp?"

Beckett squinted. "Looks like a little residential area."

Silas handed over the binoculars. "It's not residential; it's commercial. You can even see it from here."

Beckett brought the binoculars up and focused on the section of town Silas had pointed out on the map. "I see the golden arches, but I don't think we can get a Quarter Pounder anytime soon."

"Look below the McDonald's sign."

Beckett adjusted the focus. "I see a red cross, but I can't make out the words."

"It's Truckee Mountain Hospital."

Beckett nodded as he stared into the distance. "I remember that area. Isn't there a school and a grocery store?"

"And a bunch of other businesses, too. It'll take work, but if we have the chance to secure a hospital, Elias will be thanking us for years."

"You really think it'll have anything left?" Beckett handed the binoculars back. "It's been nine months."

Silas made a show of folding up the map. "It's the only major medical facility north of the interstate. It's worth a shot."

"A place like that is going to be a pain in the ass to clear. It'll take a huge team."

"We can scout it first. Go in small and light and scope

it out. If there's a ton of people, or the hospital is torched, we can regroup and pick a different spot. But I'm telling you, this is what Elias wants. That's how we build a new life."

Beckett rubbed at the gaiter covering his neck. "So we hit the hospital first and see if it's worth taking over. Then we secure the road and everything to the north."

Silas nodded. "We already own our stretch of I-80. If we take the north, we'll box in that part of town. If the hospital area has promise, we can come at it from both sides and flush people out."

"It could be the start of something new." Beckett held up his hands like he was framing a sign. "Welcome to Cunningham, California."

"Hell, it could be the Country of Cunningham for all we know."

Beckett grinned. "I like the sound of that."

Silas packed up his gear and clambered back on his snowmobile. "Let's go tell Elias."

"And eat some breakfast. If we're going on the attack, I'm not doing it hungry."

CHAPTER TWO

WALTER

Clifton Compound
9:00 a.m.

Walter blew on his hands to warm his fingers before turning the freezing knob. A red light illuminated the word ON. It had taken months of scavenging and weeks of tinkering, but he'd finally done it.

The room wasn't much: barely four by six, with unfinished lumber for walls and a single salvaged window for light. But the view through the fogged glass paled in comparison to the system of electronics bolted to the largest wall. Thanks to a largely ignored county library and a wife who knew her way around the Dewey decimal system, Walter had been able to build his own radio.

Visions of Tucker, Brianna's boyfriend, leaning over knobs and controls and teaching him the basics pinched his heart. His death seemed forever ago, even thought it hadn't been a year. Walter paused. Tucker wasn't the only casualty of this new landscape. By the time the northern states thawed in spring, there would be fewer Americans still.

He cleared his throat and leaned forward. His beard brushed the microphone, broadcasting a crackle as he began to speak.

"Good morning. This is Walter Sloane and it is the three hundredth day since a solar storm knocked out power to most of the United States. If you are listening, then you are a survivor. I know it's been a while since I've broadcast, and I apologize for the lapse."

He pulled back from the mic and glanced at the rough plywood door.

"If you are somewhere it snows, then you understand the source of my delay. The threat of a harsh winter turned this fall into a mad rush of productivity with little time for reflection. But the cruel snap of freezing temperatures has given me time to do more than survive. I've been able to learn. So here I am."

Walter swallowed. He began broadcasting just after the collapse to give people hope. But how to put it into words after all this time? He wiped his mouth.

"We are weeks away from the first signs of spring. Two months away from the one-year anniversary of the event that changed everything. Let that sink in. We've survived ten months without power, without government aid, without fresh deliveries of food and water. We've survived using our wits and our labor. It's an achievement that can't go unnoticed.

"So if you're listening, take a few minutes today to stop and celebrate. Congratulate yourself for making it this far. We aren't a nation of lazy do-nothings. We're a nation of pioneers and we're going to rebuild. This coming year will see the start of something new for all of us. I can feel it.

"Walter Sloane, signing off."

He clicked the power off and exhaled. His speech had been a little preachy and maybe too sentimental, but he couldn't help it. Walter had hope that the country could come back. It didn't have to devolve into little homesteads eking out a base level of subsistence through their own backbreaking labor.

They could form alliances. Pool resources. Bring civilization back.

Door hinges squealed behind him and Walter turned.

Colt stepped inside and tugged the door shut. "I've been looking for you for so long, I've got to piss just to warm up. Should have known you'd be out in this glorified outhouse preaching to the masses."

Walter grinned. Leave it to Colt to speak his mind. "I'm not preaching. And you can't take a leak in here so don't go getting any ideas."

Colt tugged off his gloves and blew on his hands. "Don't worry. These ski pants aren't coming off unless they're on fire." He pointed at the controls. "You finally get it all to work?"

Walter nodded. "Just broadcast for the first time."

"Did you tell the Jacobsons about it?"

"Not yet. But I can't imagine they'd have a problem with it."

Colt snorted. "They have a problem with everything, remember? One glimpse of Tracy at the hospital and they were going to pump her full of more holes than that radio has knobs."

"But they didn't."

"How's that shoulder?" Colt pointed at the area where Walter took a bullet.

"It's fine. And they said it wasn't them."

"You believe that?"

"I don't have a reason to doubt them."

Colt leaned against the bare wood wall and frowned. "Wish I could share your optimism, but so far they haven't given us much to go on."

"They gave Madison the rabies vaccine she needed and they saved Dani's life. Mine, too."

"Dani was shot *by* them, Walter. Saving her hardly builds my trust."

Walter exhaled. Colt was right to a degree, but what choice did they have? "We can't stay in this bubble forever."

"Why not?"

"Medicine, for one. If the Jacobsons hadn't maintained the hospital pharmacy, Madison would be dead by now."

Colt's lips thinned into a line. "Doesn't mean we have to do their work for them. Tracy and Larkin shouldn't be taking guard shifts over there. It's too soon."

"We owe them some gratitude." Walter flipped the switches to power off the radio equipment. "Besides, with the extra manpower, we can expand our scouting missions outside Truckee. Move on to Lake Tahoe or even Reno."

"It's been almost ten months. Those cities won't have anything left."

Walter reached for his gloves. "So we shouldn't try? Every trip into Truckee yields less and less. We haven't found decent supplies or medicine since the fall."

"So when we need medicine, we go to the hospital."

Walter leaned back on his heels. "Ben Jacobson isn't going to let us walk in there and take what we need unless we help him defend it."

Colt lapsed into silence, his brows heavy with unspoken thoughts. Walter knew trusting Ben and his family was a risk, but he didn't see another way forward. Brianna's family had been wonderful to take them in and provide shelter, but ten people on a small plot of land weren't enough to rebuild America.

Walter peered out the small window in the radio shed. The Cliftons used every inch of their five acres and quite a bit of the forest beyond, raising pigs, chickens, and a few dairy cows, along with a twenty-tree apple orchard and a smattering of other fruit trees here and there. Thanks to Madison's tireless work over the spring and summer, they had an acre of farmland that grew everything from kale and spinach in the early cool season to tomatoes and zucchini in the summer. By the fall they could harvest every kind of winter squash and another round of greens.

They could feed sixty people during a good year but only had ten. Walter knew not every year would be as bountiful as this first one, but they were squandering their opportunities. He smoothed his beard.

"We need more people, Colt. The kids..." he paused to choose his words, "are growing up. Madison is twenty and Dani's almost sixteen."

Colt groaned and ran his hand through his hair. "Don't remind me."

"They should have the same opportunities we did to have a life."

"What's wrong with right here?"

Walter didn't like to admit it, but he knew Madison wouldn't want to stay on the Clifton property forever. "They'll want boyfriends, Colt. And eventually, families."

Colt shuddered. "They'd be better off leaving the States for that."

Walter paused. After all this time, they still didn't know what it was like in other parts of the world.

"What if it's worse? What if they get to Canada and it's overrun with American refugees and the border is closed? They might never make it back home." He shook his head. "They're safer here with us and a family with options. Ben's nephews are college-age and his kids are young. We could work together and turn Truckee into a functioning town again. Rebuild."

By joining forces with the Jacobsons they could

expand their reach. They could never bring the country back to its full glory, but they could still make the new version of the US better than this.

Colt pointed to the radio. "How about you turn that back on and see if we can find a broadcast?"

Walter raised an eyebrow. "You want to change the subject that badly, huh?"

"We talk any more about Dani finding a boyfriend and I'm going to puke."

Walter cracked a smile and flicked the main power switch back on.

CHAPTER THREE

MADISON

Clifton Compound
9:00 a.m.

Madison ground her teeth together as the needle pinched her skin. "I'm glad this is the last one."

Brianna pushed the plunger all the way down and pulled the empty syringe away. "So am I." She swiped an alcohol swab across Madison's upper arm and pressed a Band-Aid over the fresh bead of blood. "Three shots over two weeks and you should be protected against the rabies virus."

"She won't ever get it?" Dani brushed her hair out of her face as she sat at the table. At almost sixteen, she was the most resourceful teenager Madison had ever met. If anyone was prepared for the apocalypse, it was Dani.

"Not this time, at least." Brianna disposed of the needle before turning to the younger girl. "As long as the virus hasn't entered a person's brain, the inoculation is effective. I grabbed a second rabies test kit from the vet so we can test Madison's blood to be sure, but I think she's good to go."

"I'll never be able to thank the Jacobsons enough."

Dani snorted. "It should be the other way around." She rubbed at the site of her healing bullet wound.

"Is it not healing well?"

"It's fine. The stitches came out without a problem. But I don't know anyone who likes getting shot."

Brianna agreed. "Tell me about it. They tried to take us out at the pharmacy, too." She turned to Madison. "I know they saved your life, but they put us through hell to do it."

Madison pursed her lips to keep from arguing. She understood Dani and Brianna's point of view. They both almost died trying to find the vaccine that saved her. But Madison couldn't help thinking about the other side. If the Jacobsons hadn't preserved the pharmacy and risked their own lives to do it, she would be in the grips of a horrible, disgusting death.

Now, thanks to the hospital pharmacy, the entire group living at Brianna's place had access to medicine they thought long gone. Not just vaccines and antibiotics, but pain relievers and suture kits, and a whole host of other medicines. She couldn't discount what that meant to them despite the rocky start to the alliance.

If they could find a way to work together, the possibilities were endless. In a few years, they might be able to move back into town. Find a way to generate electricity through harnessing the Truckee river for hydroelectric power or outfitting buildings with solar panels to catch the summer sun. With triple the people all working toward a common goal, the future was wide open.

Peyton emerged from the small pantry area and pulled out a chair next to Madison. His football-sized frame barely fit at the table, but he never complained. If anyone would agree with her, it would be him. Madison smiled and gave his arm a squeeze. "What do you think about the Jacobsons?"

His eyebrows dipped as he thought it over. "I don't know, to be honest. On the one hand, they've helped us: fixing up your dad, giving you medicine, even saving Dani after the horrible way everything went down."

"But?"

He glanced at Brianna. "We don't know what they're really after."

Madison scrunched her nose. "Who says they're after anything other than survival, same as us?"

"That's the thing, we don't know. They have way more adults than us and a bunch of kids. Your dad said they had a whole system downtown with a warehouse for processing scavenging hauls. It had heat and sleeping bags and food, the whole nine."

"So what?"

Brianna leaned back in her chair and crossed her arms. "If they're so advanced, why do they need us to guard the pharmacy? Your mom and Larkin have been working shifts there all week. I get the sense we're being used."

"And being kept in the dark." Dani scowled.

Pre-solar flare and resulting EMP, Madison would have blown her off as a typical, angry teenager, but Dani was a survivor and at this point, family. Madison trusted her judgment. She exhaled. "You really think they're double-crossing us? What for?"

Dani stuck out her hands. "For all of this. As soon as they gain our trust, they'll swoop in here and take the place for themselves. The Jacobsons might have a pharmacy, but we've got enough food stored up for three times as many families. And with the farm you all started last summer, we could feed a small town."

Madison glanced at Peyton for help. "They haven't given us any sign they want to take over. Do you really think that's what they want?"

He palmed the tabletop, spreading his thick fingers across the grains of wood. "I hope not, but Dani and Brianna are right. As of now, we just don't know. Don't you remember Sacramento? The neighborhood turned on us in minutes. They killed Wanda and burned your house down because of what? Your mom's supplies? Brianna's Jeep?"

Peyton pressed his fingertips against the table hard enough to flush his nails. "We could wake up tomorrow to an invasion and be back at square one."

Madison couldn't believe what she was hearing. Not a single one of them was willing to take the Jacobsons at face value. Was that what the world had come to? Each makeshift family was on their own, not taking a chance, not trusting anyone?

She refused to accept it. Not without proof. She was sick of doubting everyone and everything and always thinking the worst.

Madison crossed her arms, mirroring Dani's sullen vibe. "I might be wrong, but until they give us a reason not to trust them, I'm going to believe Ben and the rest of his family when they say they want an alliance."

Brianna opened her mouth to argue when the door burst open and Colt tumbled in. His coat flapped open and snow fell in clumps off his shirt. His gloveless hands were red from the cold and tears streamed from the corners of his eyes. He'd been running without regard to the weather. Madison's stomach curdled.

"What is it?" Dani sprang up, ready for action.

Colt waved them all toward the door. "Come quick. Walter found a broadcast on the radio. You need to hear it."

Without another word, Colt turned and headed back through his hurried footsteps in the snow. Madison rushed for the coats and tossed them to their rightful owners before racing to catch up with Colt's receding back.

She slowed when she reached his side. "What is it? The government? Aid? Is America coming back?"

He didn't slow or even turn to look at her. "You won't believe me unless you hear it for yourself." Colt took the steps up to the radio shed two at a time and yanked the door open.

Walter sat in front of the control wall, a pair of headphones on his head. "Dad! What is it?" Madison rushed up as the rest of the young people filed in behind her.

Her father pulled off the headphones and turned to face the sea of panting breath and wide eyes. "It's just about to restart." He flipped a switch. A baritone voice filled the crowded room.

"This is General Arnold of the new Unified States of America."

Madison swallowed.

"Rest assured our government is now fully functional and emissaries from the central planning office will be coming to your area to complete a census soon. Census workers can be identified by their yellow vests and Unified States of America ID cards. They will be escorted by senior members of the Unified Military Force."

Brianna reached for Madison's hand and squeezed. *Unified?* What did that even mean?

"We expect one hundred percent compliance. After this initial round of information-gathering, aid workers will arrive to disseminate information, rations, and potable water."

Madison couldn't believe what she was hearing. It sounded like the instructions for an internment camp or a refugee facility. Not the government of the country she'd grown up in. Not America.

"Please be patient as we complete the intake process. You will receive more information about jobs, resources, and the rule of law in the coming weeks. The Unified States of America are back and better than ever before. We must all do our part to thrive."

The recording began again and Walter shut it off.

"What the hell was that?" Brianna pushed her curls off her face, holding her head like it might explode. "Unified States of America? Is this some sort of a joke?"

"It didn't sound like a joke to me." Peyton's face paled to a color somewhere between milk and Swiss cheese. "It didn't sound like we had a choice, either."

"There should have been elections or discussions or something. They can't just make up a new country and put this general in charge." Brianna spun around in a circle. "We have rights!"

"Not anymore." Colt kept his voice even, but Madison could hear the anger behind the words. "For all we know, the president is dead and this General Arnold is in charge."

Dani wrapped her arms around her middle. "It's just like Eugene all over again."

Madison shuddered remembering the stories Dani told about Colonel Malcolm Jarvis and her narrow escape from the National Guard.

Walter held up his hands. "We don't know that. We don't know anything more than what the radio broadcast told us. There will be a census worker coming soon. We can ask him or her for information."

Brianna snorted. "Is that before or after their armed guards shoot us for insubordination?"

"We should keep an open mind."

"Like we've been doing with the Jacobsons? How do we know these yellow-vested creeps aren't just scouts reporting back what to confiscate?" Brianna palmed her forehead as she paced back and forth, her voice rising with each frantic thought. "We should hunker down and fortify our defenses. No way is some census taker getting in here and seeing what we have."

"Brianna, please." Walter tried to smile. "Let's not be rash."

She snorted. "We have to get Tracy and Larkin out of that pharmacy. They need to know what's coming."

Walter checked his watch. "I agree, but their shift is almost over. By the time we get there, we'll have missed them." He stood up. "We can rendezvous at the Jacobsons and have a two-family meeting. Tell everyone at once."

"No way!" Brianna stomped her foot. "This is exactly what Ben's been waiting for. He'll probably open the pharmacy doors and let these Unified States of America thugs come in and take it all."

"That can't happen." Colt's jaw ticked. "If we tell Ben about the radio broadcast, then we have to convince him that the census takers are a threat. We have to protect the pharmacy."

Madison chewed on her lip. There were so many unanswered questions. Did the man on the radio speak the truth? Was there really no such thing as the United States anymore? How long would it take these new workers to reach a small town in northern California? Weeks? Months?

She voiced her thoughts. "What if the census people never make it here? Truckee's a tiny town. Only sixteen thousand when it was full. They might not even come."

"We can't risk it. We have to prepare."

Brianna nodded. "Colt's right. We need to bring Tracy and Larkin home." She reached into her pocket for the Jeep's keys. "I can leave now."

Walter tugged on his coat. "I'll come with you."

"Are you going to tell Ben?" Colt stood beside the door, concern pinching his brow.

Walter hesitated. "I don't know yet."

"You should do what you think is right." Madison stepped toward her father. "If you assess the situation and you think Ben can be trusted, you should tell him."

Brianna tugged open the door. "We can decide together."

Colt nodded his head in agreement. "Fine, but be careful. Once the information is out there, we can't take it back."

Madison watched from the corner of the shed as her best friend and father rushed to the canary-yellow four-by-four. She wouldn't be able to concentrate until her family was reunited and they could talk everything over together.

Whether the radio broadcast was truthful or not, everything had changed.

CHAPTER FOUR

TRACY

Truckee Mountain Hospital

11:00 a.m.

"You think there's anything left of Hollywood?"

Tracy glanced over at John Jacobson with a sad smile. "Probably not."

The young man kicked at a scuff in the linoleum as they walked down the hall. "I was a film major in college. You know, before."

"At UNLV?"

He nodded. "Planned on moving to LA as soon as I graduated. Hollywood was a long shot, but I was willing to put in the work. Grunt jobs, waiting tables, that kind of thing." He puffed out a breath. "Seems stupid now."

"Don't say that. People always need entertainment."

"Not a lot of work in the movie industry at the moment, if you hadn't noticed."

Tracy slowed to look up at John. He towered a foot above her in height, but the more she got to know him, the more he reminded her of Peyton. Quiet, strong, humble. Peyton's father had gone the Hollywood route, turning his back on his only son to pursue his career. Fame and fortune wasn't the holy grail people made it out to be.

"What if you started writing stories? Or learned to sing?"

John stopped walking, his eyebrows screwed together like one giant caterpillar. "And what? We all put on a musical like the von Trapp Family Singers?"

Tracy laughed.

"What's so funny?"

"I was picturing us all in outfits made from curtains singing Do Re Mi."

John tucked his chin and laughed into his chest. "You don't want to see Ben in lederhosen."

The pair lapsed into silence, Tracy thinking about the future with the Jacobsons as allies and possibly more. Madison and the rest of the younger members of their group needed friends. At twenty years old, Tracy's daughter couldn't be expected to stay single and alone her entire life. She needed opportunity and the Jacobson clan provided it.

John and Daniel were good boys, about her daughter's age, and willing to put in the work to keep their families safe. Over the past two weeks, Tracy had gotten to know more of the Jacobson family, including Ben's wife Jenny and their small children. Combining forces would turn their little group of survivors into a small town.

Together, they could make something of this new life. She glanced up at John as they rounded a corner. "Thanks again for saving Madison. If your uncle hadn't given the go-ahead, she wouldn't have made it."

John rubbed at his hair. "I wish you'd stop thanking us. I still feel terrible that we tried to take you out."

"We would have done the same thing."

"How's Dani?"

"Healing up. The stitches came out yesterday. She'll have a scar, but mobility seems fine."

"Good."

Tracy pressed her lips together. She wanted more than anything to solidify the alliance between the two families. As the de facto leader, Ben Jacobson had the ultimate say, but John's word had to count for something. After another moment's hesitation, she took the plunge. "Do you think Ben will want to pool our resources?"

"You're already working shifts here."

"True. But what about the farm operations and scavenging? With all of us working together, we could expand our search areas and build something more."

"You mean like a new town?"

Tracy nodded.

John squinted down the hall like he was trying to see the future. "Logistics will be difficult. We're at least ten miles apart."

"We could use the hospital as an anchor. Clean it out and set it up as a base."

"Too risky. When it warms up, people will be all over this place."

"Then we should move all the drugs out."

"That's not my call."

Tracy picked up on the irritation in John's voice. "But you'd like to?"

John slowed as they reached the pharmacy door. He pushed it open. "Ben says it's too dangerous."

"What is?" Major James Larkin stood inside the patient waiting area, a rifle in one hand and a year-old protein bar in the other.

"Eating that, for one." Tracy's mouth turned down in disgust. "Did you scrape the mold off it, or are you keeping it on for flavor?"

Larkin grinned. "You know those best-by dates are suggestions only. This thing will last another year at least."

He was no longer a member of the US Army, but Larkin still found a way to remind everyone of his ability to handle the worst conditions. He ripped another bite off the bar before contorting his cheeks as he tried to chew. After a few agonizing moments he choked it down. "See? It's fine."

John groaned.

Tracy shook her head. "Remind me to thank Anne for her canning skills. I'd take a jar of asparagus over that dried-out brick any day."

"Then you should thank me for not dipping into her supply." Larkin wadded up the wrapper and threw it in the abandoned trash can in the corner. "So what's so dangerous Ben won't do it?"

Tracy glanced at John. The boy didn't volunteer, so she spoke up. "He doesn't want to relocate the pharmacy."

"I agree."

"You do?"

Larkin nodded. "We can't move it until the snow thaws. Too difficult to get trucks in here and load up with ice and freezing temps. But as soon as it warms, it should be priority number one."

"He'll never go for it." John perched on the edge of the intake counter. "We tried to get him to move everything over the summer. Ben wouldn't even have the discussion."

"Then we need to change his mind." Larkin motioned to Tracy. "We've got seven good shots and plenty of ammunition. With combined forces, there's no reason not to move the pharmacy unless we're clearing out the hospital to use for some other purpose."

Tracy nodded. She'd been thinking about the hospital and what they could do with it all week. With the sheer size and limited access points, it could be the start of something larger than themselves. They could consolidate everything from a library to a general store to the pharmacy and clinic all inside.

It would take months of hard work, but the hospital's location made it ideal as a home base. Sitting on the north side of the main road with only a small commercial area surrounding it, they could clear the entire area and set up a wider perimeter defense before the next year's winter.

All that space, safe from the winter elements, with plenty of natural light in the exterior rooms. Safety dictated they move the pharmacy's stash while they rebuilt, but it wouldn't be forever. Once they secured the small commercial area of town where the hospital was located, they could move it back and expand.

Tracy lifted her head with a smile. "I'm sure if we explain our thought process, Ben will understand."

John snorted. "You don't know my uncle."

The radio sitting on the counter crackled and Daniel's voice filled the room. "Daniel to base. Daniel to base. Over."

Larkin picked it up. "Base responding. Over."

"We've got movement in the north parking lot."

Tracy stiffened. With the temperatures hovering around freezing until late afternoon, they hadn't seen a single person in days.

Daniel continued. "Looks to be two scouts. Bundled up for the weather."

"Armed?"

"Rifles with scopes. They're keeping low, hugging the cars and the east parking lot wall."

Larkin turned to John. "Amateurs wouldn't do that. We're looking at people who know what they're doing."

Tracy spoke up. "What's your protocol for a situation like this?"

John slung his rifle over his shoulder and checked his pistol. "Lie low and only engage if they find a way inside."

She thought about how she and Brianna infiltrated

the hospital, convinced they hadn't been spotted. "Did you know we were coming?"

He nodded. "Saw you out in the lot. But when you didn't come in the main way, we thought you gave up. Most people do. The morgue was a surprise."

Tracy knew why. Even the memory brought back the horrifying smell. "What if they get in?"

"Then it's shoot to kill."

She shuddered. "Glad I didn't know that before."

Larkin pushed the radio button. "Give us the word when they reach inside. Until then, stay concealed."

"Roger that."

Larkin handed the radio to John. "Is the morgue secure?"

"We haven't had a chance. I can head that way. There's a spot in the parking lot with good cover where I can see the basement entrance."

"Good. Then Tracy and I will take the main hallway." Larkin held out his hand and the younger man shook it. "Good luck."

Tracy followed Larkin out the door. Ten feet down the hall, she glanced behind her, ensuring John was out of earshot before speaking. "You ready to shoot a stranger on sight?"

He glanced at her. "Not unless he gives me a reason to."

"What about John's protocol?"

Larkin made a face. "I wasn't good at following stupid orders in the Army and I'm not about to start now. We'll assess and act as needed. Hopefully they'll leave on their own and we can track them."

Tracy turned in alarm. "You want to follow a couple of armed scouts back to their place?"

He shrugged. "Apart from the Jacobsons, we haven't seen anyone worth a damn this whole winter. They could be more allies."

"Or more trouble. The Jacobsons claim not to have shot Walter, remember? What if these two are responsible? We could walk into a hornet's nest."

"Or we could find another little farm to get to know."

Tracy brought her rifle up into an easy shooting position as she walked down the hall. She was pleased about the Jacobsons, but what were the chances these new strangers were friendly? She couldn't believe Larkin's hopeful outlook. "Since when have you turned into an optimist?"

Larkin smiled wide enough to bring out the wrinkles by his eyes. "Maybe this is the new James Larkin. Open to possibility and adventure."

Tracy snorted. "Let me guess. You're just hoping for a single girl."

"Now you're catching on, Mrs. Sloane."

She shook her head as they fell into a steady walk in silence. They could talk about what to do with the strangers after they got eyes on them. If the two scouts insisted on examining the hospital, Larkin might never get the chance to find himself a date.

CHAPTER FIVE

TRACY

Truckee Mountain Hospital

1:00 p.m.

Tracy crouched beneath the glass security window to the fire door and held her breath. For the past hour, she and Larkin had waited, hoping the pair of men meticulously inching their way toward the main hospital entrance would grow weary and turn around. But luck wasn't on their side.

Daniel's voice broke through the silence on the radio. "They've split up. One is approaching the main hospital entrance, the other is weaving his way around to the morgue side."

Tracy tightened her grip on the rifle. *Change your mind. Go back.* She repeated the words over and over in her head, willing the men to leave. She didn't want to shoot them. For all she knew, they were just like her two weeks ago: desperate and out of options. What if one of their wives were injured and needed medicine? Antibiotics or a vaccine or some critical daily pill that going without meant a horrible death?

Tracy twisted around. Larkin stood guard at the other access door a hundred feet away. Apart from those two entrances, the Jacobsons had barricaded the small wing of the hospital tight. The single strip of glass above Tracy's head and its match across the hall were the only visuals this part of the hall afforded.

Daniel, located on the roof of the parking deck, was their eyes and ears on the outside. To keep the chatter to a minimum, he would only check in if he saw movement. Same for John, who hopefully was in position on the hospital's east side.

The radio crackled again, barely audible on the lowest setting. Tracy clicked the button. "Daniel?"

"One is inside. I repeat, one is inside."

Shit. Tracy rose up and squinted out the window. The hallway was clear. "Which one?"

"The heavyset guy with the beard. He walked through the front entrance."

She exhaled. "What about the other man?"

"I've lost visual."

What? Tracy steeled her voice. "Where did you see him last?"

"At the far edge of the hospital, headed to the emergency entrance." Tracy closed her eyes and mapped out the hospital in her head. If the second man made it inside, he'd be coming for Larkin.

Tracy turned and waved to catch Larkin's attention before holding up one finger and pointing it at him. *One man, headed your way.*

He raised a fist to show he understood.

Tracy twisted around and peered through the window once more. If the bearded man found his way through the labyrinth of hospital hallways and barricades, Tracy would need to defend the fire door from breach on her own. Without a visual on the other scout, Larkin had to keep his position.

Please, don't let it come to that.

The minutes ticked by and Tracy paced in front of the doors, unable to stay away from the glass for more than thirty seconds at a time. After what seemed like an eternity, she began to hope for the best. He must have found what he wanted or written the hospital off. No way he would still be searching. *We'll be all right.*

Just as she was about to call out to Larkin, the shadows in the hallway wavered. Tracy pulled back behind the glass, leaning over only far enough to see the ten feet in front of the door. Without lights, her eyes had adjusted to the near darkness, picking up the slightest hint of movement in the midday hospital gloom.

The Jacobsons had worked hard to build their defenses, propping open all the doorways outside of the barricade to let in daylight while sealing off the hallway in which Tracy now stood. For all intents and purposes, she was a shadow, a mere ghost in the gloom.

But out in the midday light, the barrel-chested man inching his way toward the firebreak was alive and in living color. Tracy's heart picked up speed, thudding loud enough to eclipse the sound of her harried breath. He hadn't given up. Instead, he'd found his way in and was headed straight for her.

Ten feet. Eight. Six. Four. Two. Tracy ducked into the dark.

The handles on the double doors rattled. The push bars on her side of the barricade shook.

Tracy pressed back tighter against the wall. *Just go away. Give up.*

After a minute of hard jerking and jiggling, the vibrations stopped. *Yes!* Tracy exhaled, about to step forward, when a blinding flash from what must have been a high-powered tactical light flooded the hall, racing to banish the safety of the dark. She turned.

Larkin was lit up like a sentry at the end of the tunnel, exposed and unprotected.

The light switched off a second later, plunging the hall back into darkness and blinding Tracy more than the light. Her pupils swelled and tried to adjust but it would take minutes to regain her vision. She was effectively blind.

Damn it.

As she blinked in rapid succession, the doors shook, a brutal, violent rattle that knocked Tracy off balance. The man on the other side stormed the doors again and again, slamming his full linebacker-sized shoulder against the seam. The hinges warped beneath the weight.

Tracy steeled herself. *I can't let him in.* If she didn't take a stand, it would be too late.

She reached for the flashlight duct taped to the receiver of her rifle and sucked in a breath. The doors shook again. Tracy swung out to face the window head on. As she clicked on the light, she brought the rifle into position.

"Identify yourself!" She shouted the words in as strong a voice as she could manage. Direct, but not hostile.

The man rose up, snorting like a bull, his shoulders bunched and tense. Sweat glinted across his forehead and dripped off his nose. Determination creased his brow as he stared down the beam of light. His nostrils flared and Tracy's lungs froze. He wasn't leaving.

As he rose up to his full height, chest heaving, a roar tore through his throat and out his mouth. *A battle cry*.

He charged the doors.

Tracy staggered back. "Stop or I'll shoot!"

The groaning of metal-on-metal drowned out her shout. He was going to force his way in and she would have to shoot him. She didn't want it to come to that.

She steadied her aim and yelled again. "Stop or I'll shoot."

The man finally stilled. "You can't shoot through the glass. It's bulletproof."

His voice was even, almost calm, despite the rapid rise and fall of his chest. Bright blue eyes stared at her from beneath unkept, wooly brows. Sweat and spittle soaked his beard, hiding his face and age from view.

"I don't want to shoot you. But if you break in, I'll have no choice."

"Then how about you save us all the trouble and let me in?"

"No."

"Then I don't see what there is to talk about."

Tracy tried again. "Why are you here?"

He snorted. "Why are you?"

"To protect something that doesn't belong to you."

"Nothing belongs to anyone anymore. To the victor goes the spoils."

"You won't be the victor."

"Don't be so sure."

Tracy lowered her head to take a shot. "Last chance."

"That's what you think." The man turned on his heel and ran down the hall before turning left at the first opportunity and disappearing from sight.

Tracy sagged, lowering the rifle to point at the floor.

"You all right?" Larkin's voice cut across the hall.

"For now." She turned toward him. "But I think he'll be back. Any sign of his friend?"

"Not yet."

Tracy tugged the radio off her belt. "Daniel? Do you copy?"

She counted to ten. No response. "Daniel? Can you hear me?" Only static.

Fear lifted the hairs on Tracy's neck. She tried the radio. "John? John do you copy?" No response.

She called out to Larkin. "Neither Jacobson is responding."

"Let's wait until check-in time. If you can't make contact with them before then, I'll go out searching."

Tracy paced back and forth for a handful of minutes, trying the radio several more times without success. It wasn't like John to go out of range. They had been trading shifts for the better part of a week and she'd learned the habits of both Jacobson men. John kept to his rounds, checking in at regular intervals. Daniel played a bit fast and loose, sometimes edging out of range of the radio for five or ten minutes. But the pair always showed up on time.

Now they were out of contact and two men were somewhere on the other side of the doors, looking for a way in. Tracy couldn't go out to search. Opening the doors was exactly what the two strangers wanted. No, as much as it pained her, they would have to wait for John and hope Daniel was out of range.

Every minute or so, Tracy checked her watch. Five, ten, then fifteen. They were late. She tried the radio again. "John? Do you copy?"

Nothing.

She clipped the huge radio back on her belt and hurried down the hall. "It's been too long. One of us needs to go out."

James Larkin propped his rifle on his shoulder and rubbed at a thin part of his beard beneath his chin. The man had more experience in combat than Tracy would ever even hear about. She trusted his judgment.

"We have to assume they're compromised."

"All the more reason to go looking for them. One of them could be hurt and need medical attention."

"Or they could both be dead and the men trying to get in are counting on us to take a chance."

Tracy ran a fingernail across her palm to focus despite the fear. "You think we stay put?"

"It's an option. When we miss a check-in at the farm, Ben will send a scouting party."

"That might take twenty-four hours." Tracy shook her head. "John and Daniel need us now."

"We don't know that for sure."

Tracy inhaled through her nose and closed her eyes. "What's more important? The pharmacy or John and Daniel?"

"To whom? 'Cause I'm going to bet the answer will differ depending on who you ask."

Tracy opened her mouth to argue when the unmistakable sound of gunfire pierced the silence. She whipped around, rifle gripped in both hands, and ran back to her guard position. The radio crackled on her hip.

"Mayday. Mayday. Tracy if you can hear me, we need help. Daniel's been shot." A rapid volley of gunfire cut off John's plea.

Tracy jammed the radio up to her mouth and clicked the button. "John! John can you hear me?"

Static was the only response.

CHAPTER SIX

WALTER

Carpenter Valley Road
    North of Truckee, CA
    1:00 p.m.

Snow blanketed the sides of the road as Brianna and Walter drove toward the Jacobson farm. Pine trees stuck up through the gray and white landscape like a thousand sentinels watching their progress in silence.

The trek between the Clifton property and the Jacobson property wasn't easy. Before the EMP, the easiest way would have been cruising down the mountain, hopping on I-80, and blowing right through the northern edge of Truckee before edging back up into the higher elevations.

But that was when snowplows and salt and continuous skier traffic kept the roads clear 24/7. Now, navigating the highway was almost impossible with abandoned cars and deep, virgin snow. It left the narrow, winding roads of the northern foothills as the only option without a snowmobile. Four-wheel drive, required.

Brianna eased the Jeep around a tight curve and climbed higher up the hill. They passed an abandoned ski lodge and Walter shook his head. "This time last year, that place would be busting from the seams with kids falling all over themselves and a million ski instructors. Now look at it."

The Closed sign hung lopsided off one metal hook and drifts of snow packed against the floor-to-ceiling windows. A solitary crow perched on the roof, stark black against the gray, frozen sludge. As they sped by, it took flight, keeping pace as the ski lodge disappeared in the rearview.

Directly south of their current location sat Truckee Mountain Hospital and the only cache of medicine Walter knew of from Nevada to Sacramento. Maybe the only one in the entire state. Ben Jacobson knew the importance of the medicine—it's why he guarded it with a rotating crew every single day. But would he see the radio broadcast as a threat or salvation?

Walter didn't know. He pinched his lower lip, rolling it between his index finger and thumb as a burned-out gas station came into view. A row of X's filled each price display on the oversized sign. Black frames of soot and char highlighted the destruction of the convenience store. Even if the power did come back on, the gas station, along with so many other businesses, would never reopen.

An old El Camino with spoke rims and a two-tone

paint job sat ten yards from the burned-out store, driver's door wide open. Snow blew across the worn leather seat, collecting against a slumped-over shape huddled against the far door. A person, or what was left of one.

Walter twisted to stare straight ahead. Millions of Americans who managed to hang on through the summer and fall in the northern states were rewarded with a brutal winter. Higher than usual snowfall, painfully cold temperatures. Those who didn't have the means to heat and feed themselves were surely dead by now.

All the more reason to take the broadcast seriously. He didn't like the tone of the so-called general's announcement or the unsaid threat of force behind it.

All laws were ultimately enforced by the barrel of a gun. It was something even his family didn't truly understand before. Before the EMP, if a citizen didn't pay yearly income taxes, one of the IRS's two thousand special agents could come in and seize assets by force. Same with environmental violations; break a rule and an EPA officer could have shown up demanding access with a gun on his hip.

There were over two hundred thousand non-Defense Department federal officers authorized to make arrests and carry firearms before the grid collapsed. More than the entire number of US Marines. Walter wondered how many of those officers were now wearing yellow vests emblazoned with the Unified States of America seal.

He knew many of his fellow Marine Corps officers would balk at a supposed general of the Unified Military Force barking orders for a government they didn't ratify.

But could the same be said for the thousands of federal agents left in limbo?

It was a question that plagued Walter from the first listen of the radio transmission up until now. Ordinarily, the longer he thought about a problem, the more sure he became about his solution. Not this time. All he knew was that the old adage applied: better safe than sorry. Convincing the Jacobsons to move the pharmacy and protect it until they learned more would be key. If Ben didn't agree...

"Hey, Walter?" Brianna snapped him out of his thoughts and he straightened up in the passenger seat.

"Yes?"

"I've been thinking about what Larkin said about Eugene and that colonel who took over the University of Oregon."

"Jarvis. What about him?"

"What if this is the same? What if a faction of the Army has taken control of the government? They could be creating new laws and putting new people in charge and we wouldn't have any say in it."

Walter nodded. "I've been thinking along the same lines. We have to assume the worst. If we're wrong, that's wonderful. But expecting these vest-wearing government workers to be benign is asking for trouble."

Brianna exhaled into a smile. "Good. I was worried you wanted to welcome them in."

Walter chuckled. "Not a chance. But I do want to tell Ben what we've learned."

Brianna stiffened and her hands tightened around the

steering wheel. "Why can't we just wait and see what happens?"

"Because we need to prepare. Ben won't move the pharmacy without a good reason. But we can't leave it in town. If a bunch of men with guns show up to confiscate what's left in Truckee, then we'll lose everything."

She thought it over. "So telling Ben means we have a chance to keep the medicine safe?"

Walter nodded. "And if need be, we can keep each other safe, too. Together we're almost thirty strong. With the weapons we have, that's a formidable line of defense."

After a few moments, Brianna conceded. "All right. I see your point, but I want to talk to Tracy and Larkin first. They might have a different opinion."

"Agreed."

Brianna slowed the Jeep as the silos for the Jacobson property came into view. She turned onto the private drive and rolled down the window before sticking her arm out to wave at Craig. He hustled from his position as a lookout for the road and unlocked the gate.

As it swung wide, Brianna eased the Jeep forward and parked beside an old farm truck. As Walter emerged from the passenger side, a gaggle of kids ranging in age from two to ten rushed out from between two rolled bales of hay, whooping and hollering.

A snowball flew past his face and smashed against the windshield.

"Hey, I just cleaned that this morning!" Brianna palmed her hips in mock disapproval as a another snowball splatted in front of her feet. She laughed and scooped it up, mashing more snow around it. "Who did that? I swear I'm going to get you!" She took off, running for the kids who were now screaming in glee.

One of the younger girls giggled and ran toward Walter, wrapping her arms around his leg and using him as a shield. He smiled. "How are you today, Lilly?"

"I'm great! Momma said we did such a good job with chores we can take the rest of the afternoon off!"

"Good job working so hard."

She beamed up at him, blue eyes bright and shining in the frosty air. "Are you here to see Daddy?"

Walter nodded. "Do you know where he is?"

"In the big barn. He's cleaning rifles." The little girl shrieked as a snowball smashed against Walter's thigh. She took off running, blonde braids flying behind her.

Walter stood and watched for a minute longer, enjoying the sight and sounds of childhood happiness. A sudden pang of longing hit him and he choked back a wave of emotion. This was what they were missing at the Clifton farm. The unabashed joy of children. If the country was going to survive, the Jacobson family couldn't be the exception. It needed to once again be the norm.

Walter clenched his fist. Madison, Peyton, Brianna, and Dani deserved to have this chance. They needed the Jacobson alliance more than any of them wanted to admit. He wiped his mouth and strode toward the large red barn. A faded American flag was painted above the sliding door and as Walter headed toward it, the door opened.

Ben Jacobson emerged, wiping his bare hands on a greasy rag. Stout and burly, Ben Jacobson looked every bit the working-man in his overalls and boots. He smiled and his beard curved. "Walter Sloane. To what do I owe the pleasure?"

Walter shook the man's hand and motioned toward the open door. "Is Tracy inside?"

Ben shook his head. "They're not back yet."

"But it's past the shift change, isn't it?" Walter checked his watch in alarm. Tracy and Larkin should have arrived and been fueling up with a hot meal. "Have you heard anything?"

"Our radios don't have that kind of range. I'm sure it's nothing. Sometimes the boys find something on the way home and scout it out. Last week Daniel almost sent Heather into cardiac arrest when he didn't come home by dinner. Turns out he found a stray cow and was trying to shepherd it into the back of the truck."

"Did it work?"

Ben nodded. "She's in the cattle pen now. Looks to be a good milker, too."

Walter exhaled and tried to slow the beating of his heart. Ben was right. There were a million reasons for the delay. He didn't need to rush to worry. He glanced behind him, looking for Brianna. She, along with the Jacobson children, were gone.

They couldn't wait on Tracy and Larkin to tell Ben the truth. Despite Brianna's reservations, Ben needed to know. Walter hoped she would accept his decision. He turned back around. "Can we talk?"

"Sure." Ben tucked his rag into his bib pocket. "Is there a problem?"

"That depends on your definition of problem, I suppose." Walter followed Ben toward the barn, rehearsing in his head how he would explain what they had heard. If Ben didn't agree to move the pharmacy, or worse, opted to welcome the new government with open arms, Walter and the rest of the Clifton group had a decision to make. One that might not only destroy the tenuous alliance with the Jacobson clan, but start a war.

CHAPTER SEVEN

TRACY

Truckee Mountain Hospital
2:00 p.m.

Tracy's heart pounded against her ribs as she struggled to make a decision. They couldn't leave John and Daniel out there to die. But the medicine could save so many more than two lives.

Sweat broke across her upper lip, stinging her chapped skin as she licked it away. "We have to go. We have to find them."

Larkin glanced at the fire doors. "Will they hold?"

"That guy slammed into them at least ten times. Unless he comes back with a battering ram, I think so."

"All right." Larkin jerked his head toward the stairwell. "We'll go out through the morgue. If we can barricade it up, we should be able to find John and Daniel and make it back before anyone breaks in."

"What if they need medical attention?"

"Let's worry about finding them first. For all we know, they're both dead." Larkin cut-off the conversation, turning away from Tracy as he strode toward the stairwell. He lowered into a crouch and with a grunt, pushed the metal desk blocking the door to the stairs out of the way. "We won't be able to replace the desk, so we'll have to figure something out downstairs."

Tracy nodded and followed Larkin into the darkness. As the door shut behind her, she clicked on the flashlight strapped to her rifle.

Larkin called over his shoulder as he descended the flight. "Do you remember how to get out down here?"

"The stairs open to a hallway, but it's crowded. We'll have to snake our way through to the main receiving bay and out the door."

"Crowded with what?"

Bile rose up Tracy's throat. "You'll see."

Larkin stopped at the door and checked his rifle before aiming a foot on the release bar. The door swung open and he gagged. "*Damn*. You should pull up your shirt. It's ripe down here."

"I remember." Tracy sucked in the last breath of stale but palatable air and followed Larkin into the morgue. It was worse than she remembered.

The desperation of that day came back with the smell. She and Brianna found the hospital, hoping beyond all hope that a rabies vaccine might still be inside. But they couldn't reach the pharmacy and frustration, anger, and overwhelming sadness had all combined to push them forward, ignoring the reality of the situation.

But she couldn't avoid it now. Every sweep of her tactical flashlight illuminated another horror. Gurneys heaped with five, six, seven bodies, most rotted down to strips of tendon and bone. Body bags stuffed to the breaking point stacked one on top of each other all along the length of the hallway.

Larkin turned to face her. "Did we have a pandemic and I missed it?"

Tracy covered her face with her forearm to block the smell. "When the hospital's generators failed, the critical patients would have died within hours. Truckee's not large, but this is the nearest hospital for lots of small mountain towns. They could have had hundreds of inpatients."

"There's more than a hundred bodies here."

"That was only the beginning. Think about all the elderly people in the area. The sick who needed monthly medicine. All the people who ran out of food or water." She shuddered. "A coworker of mine lived in a retirement community. Within a day it was an above-ground graveyard."

Tracy lowered the rifle to the floor, lighting a single, filthy square of linoleum as she thought of Wanda and those early days. All the elderly people on oxygen who died when the generators failed. The thieves who took advantage before the bodies were even cold.

Her own neighborhood had gone from quiet and

peaceful to anarchy in less than a week. What was it like now? Were any of her neighbors even alive?

"Which way?"

Tracy shook off the past and jerked her rifle back into position. "Straight ahead. The hall opens into the receiving area. We can get out the emergency exit door beside the automatics. Those are locked."

Larkin turned around. The flashlight beam reflected off the floor to light his face from below like a ghost haunting the dead. "We need something to block the entrance. Make it look like no one's been here since the hospital fell."

Although Tracy's stomach heaved at the thought, she pointed at the closest gurney. "One of those should work."

Larkin nodded and slung his rifle over his back before tugging his shirt up over his nose. He approached the closest cart and kicked off the foot brake. As he pushed against the handle, a desiccated arm slipped off the side. Something metal clanged to the floor and Tracy bent to pick it up.

A wedding ring.

Solid gold with a single diamond in the center, it symbolized someone's love. She swallowed hard. If Walter hadn't found them on the road to Brianna's place, Tracy or Madison could look like that now. A pile of bones unable to hold onto what mattered.

She set the ring on the edge of the cart and helped Larkin push it into position and lock the wheels. It wouldn't keep someone determined out, but it might mask the way upstairs.

Larkin stepped back and shined his light across the door. He stopped on the sign for the stairs. "We should pry that off." He dug a multitool out of his pocket and set to work, wedging it between the sign and the wall. It popped off, leaving a jagged spot of glue on the paint. "Good enough. Let's go."

Together, they made their way through the morgue and out into the bitter cold. They stopped behind an abandoned ambulance and caught their breath.

The fresh air shocked Tracy's senses and her eyes watered as she fumbled with her sunglasses and coat. "John was stationed in the parking deck on the other side of the hospital. We should go there first."

"We can scout for Daniel on the way. He should have headed north to Emergency and around to the parking deck. If he's not out here, then we have to hope they're hunkered down in the deck." Larkin brought his rifle up and held it tight against his shoulder. "I'll lead. You see anyone, don't hesitate to shoot."

Tracy frowned. They still didn't know what happened or who the two men were or what they wanted. For all they knew, they could be innocent. Was the man who tried to break in desperate or merely opportunistic? She had no idea. But what mattered was finding Daniel and John before it was too late.

She followed Larkin around the ambulance, staying close to the side of the building and beneath the unruly row of hedges lining the sidewalk. The front entrance loomed ahead with an oversized awning for cars to drive under and unload. No sign of Daniel or John.

They passed the front entrance and Larkin crouched behind a cluster of small pine trees. The deck sat straight ahead.

Three steps away from the trees, Larkin froze. He stuck up a hand and Tracy panned up. On the top level of the deck, a figure hunched behind a late-model sedan. Bushy, red hair stuck up all over on the man's head and Tracy assumed he must be the second scout.

Larkin brought his rifle into position and bent to take aim.

Tracy hurried up to him. "What are you doing?"

"What does it look like?"

"That you're about to shoot a man who could be completely innocent."

Larkin scoffed. "I'm eliminating a threat."

"For all we know, he's hiding from the shooter, too."

"Then he should hide better." Larkin lowered his head again.

"We can't just shoot him. Not until we're sure he's dangerous."

While they argued, the man shuffled back and forth behind the car, peering through the windows. Tracy hadn't spotted a gun. "Didn't the two scouts have rifles with scopes? If so, where is it?"

As Larkin turned to respond, the man's head swiveled their way. He didn't hesitate. The rifle swung up from out of sight and as Tracy and Larkin dove for the trees, the man fired a series of shots. Larkin hit the ground hard and rolled over onto his belly. "Is that enough confirmation for you? Or do you want me bleeding from a gunshot wound before we fire?"

Tracy hunkered down beneath the next tree, all her indecision gone. "Shoot him."

"Finally." Larkin rose up on his elbows, propping the rifle on a rock in front of him. He exhaled and pulled the trigger three times in rapid succession. The man fell backward out of his crouch and after a moment, sagged to the concrete. Larkin stood up with a grimace. "Let's find John and Daniel."

"What about the other scout?"

"Shoot to kill."

Tracy scrambled up and peered across the paved entrance. Fifty feet separated their current position and the entrance to the parking deck. With no cover, they would be exposed for the entire run. She motioned to the deck. "You go first. I'll cover you."

Larkin frowned. "Walter would never let me hear the end of it." He gave her a nudge. "You go first. I'll be right behind."

"Fine, but hurry." Tracy took one last look around before bursting from the trees in a sprint. She reached the safety of the deck without incident and turned to wave Larkin on. He followed and together, they panted hot bursts of steam into the air.

"We'll clear it floor-by-floor. If John and Daniel are here, we'll find them."

Tracy nodded and followed Larkin into the deck. It was agonizing work, searching behind, in, and under every car. But after what seemed like an eternity, they found John Jacobson. He sat, spread-eagle, against the tire of a Chevy pickup with missing trim, clutching his belly. His fingers were soaked in blood.

"Oh, no." Tracy rushed to his side while Larkin stood guard. "John? John can you hear me?" She felt for a pulse. Weak. Erratic. She pulled a handkerchief out of one pocket of her cargo pants and lifted his hand out of the way. A fresh gush of blood pumped from his wound and she pressed the cloth against it to staunch the flow.

His cheeks were lifeless, almost gray, and his lips were distinctly blue. Tracy patted his shoulder. "John? Can you hear me?" She lifted an eyelid. No dilation, no response.

"That's a hell of a lot of blood."

"Too much." She reached for his neck and found the feeble beat of his heart once more. With every pump of blood, it slowed. It couldn't have taken more than a minute to stop. Tracy leaned back on her heels and stopped pressure on the wound. She looked up at Larkin.

He didn't need to hear the words. He cursed and shook his head. "We need to find Daniel."

Tracy searched around John's body for the radio. She found it still wedged in his palm. His lifeless fingers offered no resistance when she picked it up. "Daniel? Daniel can you read me?"

Nothing but static. If he was shot first, they might already be too late.

CHAPTER EIGHT

SILAS

Truckee Mountain Hospital
    3:00 p.m.

The emotional chick with the shy trigger finger stood up and wiped the dead man's blood off her hands. Silas spat on the ground. Sentimentality got people killed. That or stupidity. He glanced over at the body of his cousin, Beckett. Idiot had been hiding in plain sight.

If Silas had his way, he'd leave the kid's body for the stray dogs and wild animals managing to hang on through the winter. But Elias would have his head for abandoning a Cunningham. Silas frowned. Beckett's death complicated things.

He couldn't go home until he had information to appease his uncle. Otherwise, he might get a fate worse than Beckett. Elias didn't appreciate failure and tended to take it out on those left standing. He glanced back at the unlikely pair of guards and thought it over. He would have to find out what was so important to barricade up the hospital and defend it. Only then could he head home.

Silas watched as the soccer mom and her military boyfriend fanned out to search the parking deck. *You better hurry, suckers.* When they were gone from sight, he eased back into the shadows and lit a cigarette. He sucked down a drag and blew the smoke into the darkness.

As he stubbed out the last of the embers, the pair returned. The man carried a lump of a body over his shoulder and the woman led, rifle up. Silas snorted. If he didn't have the military guy to contend with, Silas would kill them now and save himself some later trouble.

But he'd seen the man in action, shooting from a concealed position and taking out Beckett even under fire. If he attacked now, the man would probably use the kid as a shield. No, it was better to let them go and have all the time in the world to search the hospital.

Besides, leaving them alive gave his uncle someone to hate. An enemy he could unleash his full wrath upon that didn't have the same last name. Silas much preferred that option. He leaned against the concrete wall and let the cold seep through his jacket and into his bones.

The pair of guards hauled the wounded third man into the back seat of a pickup truck and the woman climbed in with him. She pushed her hood back and sunglasses up and Silas blinked. Older than he thought.

Practically middle-aged. He ticked a few more points into her column.

Not that it mattered. Soon enough they would learn what happens when you declare war against the Cunningham clan.

The truck engine grumbled to life and Silas watched it exit the parking lot to head north toward the ski lodges. *Interesting*. Maybe there was more than just abandoned resorts up in the foothills. He made a note to check out the area after dealing with the hospital.

With one guard dead and three on the road, Silas walked over to his cousin. Beckett lay slumped against the concrete, his blood congealing in the cold air like pudding. He took a deep breath and hoisted Beckett's body onto his shoulder before turning toward the stairs. Taking them as fast as an added two hundred pounds would allow, Silas hustled down the flight.

Their snowmobiles were hidden at the entrance to the parking lot behind an abandoned bus and Silas headed straight there, not stopping until he deposited Beckett's body on the back of the rig. Using a tarp tucked in the saddlebag of his vehicle, Silas wrapped his cousin's body and lashed it to the rear of the seat. It wouldn't be the prettiest procession back home, but dead men didn't get a say in the land of the living.

Beckett could pound him for the rough treatment when they met again in the hereafter. Silas closed his eyes for a moment and sent up a prayer. It was all he could do for now.

Now the hospital. Silas fished his hatchet out of his

saddlebag along with a smoke grenade and a backup handgun and stuffed them all into various pockets in his parka. If there were more guards hiding inside, he would be ready.

Five minutes later, he stood back outside the doors he'd tried to breach hours before. Slamming into the doors had decorated them with shoulder-height dents, but they hadn't given way. He needed something that could break the lock.

Silas pulled out the hatchet and wedged it between the doors just above the locks. With all of his strength, he brought his foot down on the handle. Something inside the doors cracked. He kicked it again. The hatchet shimmied to the floor.

He rocked it out of the crack between the doors and sheathed it before giving them a push. They bowed and Silas grinned. *I can work with that.* With a deep breath and a ten yard running start, he threw his body at the dented door. It gave way and he stumbled through and into a dark hall.

From his right pocket he pulled a Glock 17 equipped with the best Streamlight thieving would allow. He toggled it on and panned the hall. No noise. No movement.

He pulled the smoke grenade from his pocket with his left hand and held it low and ready. Every three steps, he panned the hall. The light was bright enough to illuminate everything within a twenty foot radius, but that didn't mean he was safe. The guards had been crafty.

Sealing off this side of the hospital meant lower visibility for intruders.

Presumably, soccer mom and her friends knew the area even in the complete darkness. It would give them an advantage in every fight. Silas crept down the hall to the first door. He jiggled the handle. Waited. Opened the door.

Nothing. He eased inside and closed it behind him before lighting up the space.

About ten chairs sat in groups around coffee tables in the main area, clearly rearranged for current use. Behind them stretched a counter with signs for pickup and drop off and a cash register to the right. Silas blinked.

You've got to be shitting me.

He stepped forward. The shelves were full. It was a stocked hospital pharmacy. He almost laughed out loud. Elias would never believe it. Silas could go home, explain until he was blue in the face, and Elias would order him out of the room and tell him to sleep it off. He looked around him.

I have to prove it.

If he could convince Elias that the pharmacy was fully loaded, Beckett's death would be an afterthought. They would send an army of Cunninghams down to capture the hospital and stake their claim over the entire area. Hell, Silas might get the whole town named after him.

He hopped the counter and searched in the cabinets until he found plastic bags. He loaded them up with as many drugs as he could carry, not worrying about what they were, just whether he could get them all to fit. When he'd filled them all, he tied the bags shut and used an extra to lash them all together.

After hoisting the collection over his shoulder, Silas backtracked through the waiting area and out the pharmacy door. Before the door shut, he paused. A grin puffed out his beard and he reached into his pocket for the hefty black cylinder.

He set the bags on the floor, and headed back into the pharmacy. After finding a roll of KT tape, he unrolled three strips and used them to adhere the cylinder to the doorjamb.

Once he ensured the tube was secure, he popped the top on the cylinder and affixed another strip of tape to the side of the door. After easing out of the room, he slipped the tape strip through the metal pull on the top of the tube and smoothed it across the door as it swung shut. Not the easiest maneuver with meat-stick fingers, but he managed all right. Besides, the weight of the door would seal the tape and hold the metal ring in place.

At least until one of the guards came back.

Silas smiled. He wished he could be there to see it, but he had more pressing concerns. With the bags of drugs back over his shoulder, he headed out into the freezing air and straight for his snowmobile. With a bungee cord, he lashed the drug bags to Beckett's tarp-wrapped body and slid onto the seat.

He gave his load a pat. "Don't worry, cousin. You didn't die in vain. The town of Truckee is about to be reborn."

The snowmobile revved to life and under the weight of his grip, the machine lurched forward toward Donner Lake Motor Court and his waiting uncle. Once Silas showed him the bounty and explained all that was left behind, Elias would be singing his praises. Beckett's death would be forgiven and the Cunningham clan would prepare for the start of a whole new life.

CHAPTER NINE

WALTER

Jacobson Farm

    3:00 p.m.

"That's the gist of it." Walter rubbed the back of his neck and waited for Ben's reaction. The leader of the Jacobson farm remained silent and stoic; his wife, not so much.

"We can't trust it. For all we know it could be a coup or a military faction that's gained control." Jenny Jacobson chewed on her lower lip and shook her head. "We didn't vote for a Unified States of anything."

Before Walter could explain to Ben in private about the radio transmission, Jenny, Brianna, and the rest of the family had barged in the doors, red in the face from a snowball fight across the farm. After the older kids took the younger ones back to the main house, Walter explained the story all while fielding a hostile stare from Brianna.

She spoke up as soon as Jenny finished. "Assuming these census workers show up in Truckee, we should make ourselves scarce. The less they know about us, the better."

"What if they bring supplies?" Heather Jacobson focused on her uncle. "We've been lucky so far, but if what this General Whatever-His-Name-Is said is true, they could have trained doctors and nurses. They could bring back essential services like the hospital." She glanced around the large multipurpose room. "God knows I could use the help."

Heather had treated more than just her own family over the past two weeks. Thanks to her medical training, Dani was alive and Walter's gunshot wound was almost healed. If the Jacobsons had been through even a quarter of what his group had suffered, Heather must have been exhausted. It made sense she would hold out hope.

Not everyone felt the same way. Craig Jacobson shook his head. "I don't trust it. It could all be a scam. If we welcome them, they could confiscate all the drugs and leave us to fend for ourselves." He ground his fist into his palm. "No way we let them into the pharmacy."

Brianna stepped forward. She may have been young, but she was more than capable of assessing a threat. "If we leave the pharmacy as is, we won't have a choice. They'll search the place and demand entry." She glanced at Walter, looking for support.

He nodded. "It doesn't matter if it *is* some branch of a new government. As soon as they see what you have, they'll take it. You should move the medicine."

"Don't you think that's a little rash?" Heather brushed her long hair over her shoulder and turned toward Brianna and Walter. "We spent weeks clearing and securing the hospital. Abandoning it now makes no sense."

"So you want to lose everything?"

"I don't think it will come to that."

Brianna cursed beneath her breath. "Then you're even more naïve than I thought."

Heather tried to placate Brianna with a smile. "If they're coming from any kind of distance, the snow and ice will slow them down. You know as well as I do that the roads are impassable without four-wheel drive. We probably have until the spring to make a decision."

"Or they might show up tomorrow in Humvees with guns mounted on the back. You seriously want to wait months to do anything?"

"It's an option."

"A bad one." Brianna tossed her blonde curls and cracked her knuckles.

Walter held his breath. He knew that look in her eye. Things were about to get tense.

"The Unified States of America? That's not the start of something good, it's a declaration of war." Brianna barely kept her voice above a shout. "If the military has taken over operation of the country, we're not America as we knew it. We're something else. Something dangerous. Our friends were in Eugene when the National Guard swept into that town and took over. It was horrible."

"Brianna's right." Walter waited until most eyes were

on him. "Colonel Jarvis showed up with a lot of the same promises about food and aid and rebuilding. But it quickly turned into a forced occupation with work camps and family separations and the confiscation of all weapons. Good people died."

Craig bristled. "We're not giving up this farm and going to work in some labor camp."

"But you're willing to give up the medicine you've fought for all this time?" Brianna's composure teetered. "That's ridiculous."

Ben spoke up for the first time. "Jarvis was an isolated incident. The transmission you all heard didn't originate in Oregon."

"We don't know—" Brianna interrupted, but Ben held up his hand.

"I agree. Calling it the Unified States is concerning, but we don't know the facts. These could be patriotic Americans trying to rebuild the country just like us."

"Or it could be a ruse designed to take our food and weapons and turn us into indentured servants."

Ben leaned back in his chair. "Talking in circles will get us nowhere. Let's put it to an initial vote. All those in favor of talking to these census workers, raise—"

A frantic, repetitive honking drowned out the rest of Ben's words and he jumped up from the table. Craig beat him to the door, yanking it open before disappearing into the sunshine.

Walter rushed to follow, squinting against the hard light as one of the Jacobson pickup trucks bounded into the open field. The passenger-side door flew open as the truck skittered to a stop in a weedy patch of gravel.

Please, don't let Tracy be hurt. It wasn't the kindest thought, but in the moment, it was all Walter could think. They had been through so much already. He wasn't prepared for another catastrophe. How lucky could they continue to be?

As he strained to see, holding his hand up to cast a shadow across his face, Tracy emerged from the truck and waved her arms over her head. "We need a gurney! Hurry!"

Craig took off for the medical building with Brianna on his heels while Heather and Walter closed the distance to the truck. Larkin climbed down from the driver's side and motioned for Walter's attention.

Walter wanted to get to his wife, but she was on the other side, leaning over the seat with Heather. He let Larkin lead him a few steps away. "What happened?"

Larkin dropped his voice barely above a whisper. "We were attacked. Pair of scouts with scoped rifles and snowmobiles. Obviously trained."

Walter looked beyond him to the truck. Craig and Brianna double-timed a gurney up to the passenger-side door as Ben approached.

"Who's hurt?"

"Daniel's been shot. Single gunshot wound to the side. He's unconscious. Lost a lot of blood."

"Damn it."

"That's not the worst of it." Larkin swallowed. "John's dead."

"*What?*" Walter hissed the word. "How?"

"Shot while on lookout. He died before we could find him."

Walter rubbed a hand down his face. Ben would be furious. If Daniel died too... He shook his head to stop the what-ifs. "Are you and Tracy hurt?"

"No. We got one of the shooters. Big guy, early twenties. Looked like he'd been in the mountains a while."

"You said there were two."

Larkin nodded. "Thought it was better to get Daniel back here instead of hunting the other one down."

"What about the pharmacy?"

"It's as secure as we could manage. The fire doors were holding. We barricaded the door in the morgue." He glanced behind him as Ben and Craig carried Daniel's unconscious form away from the truck and toward the medical building. Brianna and Heather followed.

Tracy rushed toward Walter.

He wrapped his arms around her. "Thank God you're all right."

"I wish I could say the same for John and Daniel."

"Larkin filled me in." Walter pulled back. "You're sure it was only two?"

His wife nodded. "But they must have come from a group. Well-running vehicles and plenty of fat around the middle." She shuddered. "They were strong, too."

Walter didn't like the look on her face. Based on her grimace, he was even more thankful she made it out of there alive. This changed everything about the pharmacy discussion. "Ben will have to see reason."

"About what?"

"Moving the drugs. This attack combined with the radio transmission—he'll have no choice."

Tracy's eyebrows lifted. "What radio transmission?"

Walter exhaled. He forgot his wife and Larkin didn't know. In as few words as possible, he laid out what it said.

Larkin bristled. "'Unified States' my ass. No way are any supposed census workers taking a step on our turf."

"I'm sure Anne and Barry will see it that way, but Ben might not agree." Walter looked toward the medical building. "Ben's been waiting all this time for the government to stitch itself back together. If he thinks this is it, he might welcome these workers in."

"And get rounded up like everyone in Eugene?" Larkin almost spat on the ground. "You know what happened there. So many good people died because of Jarvis and his quest for control. If they do the same thing here, we'll all be turned into glorified slaves or taken out back and shot."

He ran a hand over his sandy-blond hair and turned around in a circle as if he could find the answer on the ground. "If the Jacobsons roll over, can we trust them not to rat us out? For all we know they'll lead these people right to us."

Tracy spoke up. "We can't worry about that now. What matters is the pharmacy. That man will be back. And the next time, he'll be ready."

Walter exhaled. They had to convince Ben to move the drugs if it wasn't already too late.

CHAPTER TEN

TRACY

Jacobson Farm

   5:00 p.m.

The icy winter wind dried the sweat and dirt on Tracy's face into a gritty paste. She wiped at her eyes as she turned to face her husband. "We have to convince Ben to move the pharmacy now."

Walter nodded. "I know. But first, we have to tell him his nephew is dead."

Larkin groaned. "If they don't move the pharmacy, then his death and the countless man-hours spent guarding the place will all be for nothing."

As Tracy opened her mouth to agree, Ben emerged from the medical building. He hunched against the weather as he made his way to their group huddled by the F-150. Tracy held her breath, preparing to break the terrible news.

"How is Daniel?" She managed a small smile.

"Heather kicked me out. Said I was too big to help." Ben rubbed at his beard. "We won't know for a while."

"I know you're not ready to hear this, but I have more bad news."

Ben stilled. "About the men who did this?"

She shook her head. "About John. There's no good way to say this."

Larkin stepped up. "He's dead."

"What?" Ben took a step back. "How?"

"Gunshot wound to the gut."

Ben closed his eyes. After a moment, he turned to Larkin. "Walk me through it."

Larkin relayed what happened from first seeing the two men, to John losing visual, to the one attacking Tracy's door, and John radioing for help. When he reached the part of the story where they found John, he faltered.

Tracy continued. "Larkin shot one of the scouts—not the man who attacked my door, but the other one. Probably the shooter. He died instantly."

"Good." Ben snuffed back wave of snot and emotion. "What about Daniel?"

"We found him behind a vehicle in the parking deck. He was unconscious, but still alive. We rushed him to the truck and drove straight here."

"So who's watching the pharmacy?"

"At the moment? No one."

Ben cursed. "That goes against every protocol we have! If I knew your group would be this sloppy—"

Larkin cut him off. "Would you rather us bring you two dead nephews or one? Tracy had to apply pressure to Daniel's wound and I had to drive. It was leave the pharmacy and try to save him, or watch him die and wait for the shift change."

Walter held out his hands. "It was a high-stress moment. I'm sure they did the best they could, John and Daniel included."

Ben began to pace, striding back and forth in a ten-foot strip of slushy gravel. After a few moments, he came back to the group. "What about the other man?"

Tracy winced as she broke the news. "He's loose. For all we know he's back at his camp, assembling a crew to break in."

Ben turned as the door to the medical building opened and Brianna and Craig stepped out. "We need someone out there."

"We need to move the medicine." Tracy spoke as calmly as she could manage. "If we don't move it, we'll lose more people. The barricades won't hold against a coordinated attack."

"She's right, Ben." Walter nodded at his wife. "Even if my whole group sets up a line of defense, we can't protect the pharmacy from a military-style attack. It's too risky."

Ben's shoulders sagged. It took him a minute to answer. "I don't like it, but I see your point. Let's head back to the barn and draw up plans." He turned to Brianna and Craig as they joined the group. "We're moving the pharmacy."

"It's about time." Brianna crossed her arms.

"We need people out there covering it until we're ready."

"I'll go." Brianna reached into her pocket and pulled out the Jeep's keys.

"So will I." Craig reached out and gave his uncle's shoulder a squeeze. "We'll protect it until you get there."

"We'll head out first thing in the morning." Ben turned to the rest of the group. "Let's get in and figure out what to do. Now."

Clifton Compound

9:00 p.m.

Tracy wrapped the flannel tighter around her shoulders as she stood on the porch to the sleeping cabin. Walter eased the door shut behind him before handing her a mug of steaming tea. She took it with a sad smile.

"Penny for your thoughts."

"I don't like Ben's plan." She blew on the hot liquid before taking a sip. "First Brianna goes to the pharmacy, now Colt and Madison. The kids should have stayed here."

"What if that guy comes back? They need the firepower at the hospital."

"I should be there."

"No. You pulled a twenty-four-hour shift and almost

got yourself killed. You need rest." Walter sipped his own tea. "If anyone should be there, it should be me."

"You have to go with Ben. He listens to you."

"About the medicine or the radio broadcast?"

"Both. That medicine is important not just to the Jacobsons, but to us, too. I know they've been protecting it, but we have just as much of a right to it as they do. It's not theirs."

"But it's not ours, either."

Tracy sighed. "That doesn't mean we should let some guy claiming to represent the government take it. Or leave it in the pharmacy where these new people can break in and steal it."

"Agreed."

"We have to stand up for ourselves."

Walter wrapped an arm around his wife. "Have I told you lately that I love you?"

She smiled. "I never get tired of hearing it." She sipped her tea again and leaned against the comfort and solidity of her husband's body. "No matter what happens, we have to keep our family safe. That's the priority."

"And the Jacobsons?"

"God willing, they'll be safe, too." She thought about Madison and her brush with death. The crisis and panic Tracy felt inside as she searched for a rabies vaccine and came up empty was overwhelming. Grace and luck brought her to the hospital and the Jacobsons made it possible to save her daughter. They couldn't give it all away now or let it fall into the wrong hands. She snuggled closer. "We need that medicine, Walter."

"Madison will be okay, even if we lose the pharmacy."

"But what kind of a future will she have?" John wasn't much older than Madison and he was dead. Daniel clung to life thanks to Heather and their medical supplies. Any one of them could come face-to-face with death at any moment.

Walter tightened his embrace. "She'll have the best future we can give her."

"I hope that's enough."

Her husband exhaled. "Do you remember the first day we dropped Madison off at kindergarten?"

Tracy leaned back to catch her husband's face. "Of course. I remember walking up to the trailer and thinking we had to be lost. I couldn't believe they would put the kindergartners in a rundown mobile home because of overcrowding."

The school had been redistricted that summer and found itself over capacity with no means to house all the elementary classes. The temporary classroom trailers borrowed from another school weren't fit to house farm animals, let alone children.

"But what happened when we picked her up?"

Tracy smiled. "We couldn't get her to leave. Madison was gluing drawings the class made to the wall because she wanted to make her teachers smile."

"Exactly. If anyone can find the good in dark times, it's our daughter."

"What if a positive outlook isn't enough? If Ben agrees to hand everything over to the Unified States of

America or whatever it is, then everything we've worked for these past nine months might be lost."

"We'll convince him not to, but first, we have to move the medicine. That's the priority."

Tracy kissed her husband and watched him head back inside to the warmth of wool blankets and sound construction. As the door shut, she turned back around to look out over the Clifton property. She couldn't see much in the dark, but she knew the layout.

They had turned a vacation spot into a home for not just one family, but three. Ten people working and living and surviving without anyone to answer to but themselves. Nine months without a government imposing its own rules and regulations. No police, no firefighters, no taxes. Nothing but the effort of their bodies and their minds and the strength of their convictions to keep them alive.

How would Madison, Brianna, and the rest of the young people react to a new government imposing itself on their freedom? They were so independent now. Tracy thought back to life before the EMP. Teachers and coaches and bosses and police. Everyone telling them what to do every second of the day.

It wouldn't be easy to integrate back into a working nation. But if it meant safety and security and a chance to go back to life before, would they concede? She thought about all they had lost. Music, art, and movies. Great restaurants and beautiful gardens. Electricity and running water.

In a way she was happier with this simpler way of

life, but they gave up so much to have it. With a deep breath she turned to head inside. This couldn't be the best it would ever get. Life had to improve, even if it took a few sacrifices to achieve it.

She pulled the door open and eased into the comfort of the cabin. In the morning, they would head to the pharmacy and hope her daughter and the rest of their makeshift family were still safe inside the hospital walls.

301 DAYS WITHOUT POWER

CHAPTER ELEVEN

WALTER

Mountain Lake Road
8:00 a.m.

"Can't you hold it?" Walter careened into the U-Haul's passenger door and grunted.

"You want to swap?" Larkin gripped the steering wheel with white knuckles. "'Cause I'm happy to give you the reins."

Walter rubbed his shoulder where it slammed into the window. "Just slow down. If we end up in a ditch, there's no way to dig it out."

"We should never have agreed to this plan." Larkin kept his eyes on the road as the back tires of the fourteen-foot truck spun in the snow. "It would have taken more trips, but four-by-fours were the way to go."

"It would take too long. For all we know, those guys

are on their way with guns and ammo and eager trigger fingers."

"Or we took out fifty percent of their crew and the one guy left standing isn't eager for a repeat."

The rear tires slipped and the U-Haul drifted sideways. Larkin cursed and took his foot off the pedals. He eased the steering wheel to the left, turning the tires against the skid. The truck slowed as its right tire edged into the thicker snow bank and Larkin regained control.

"At this rate, it'll take all day to get there."

"We don't have a choice."

"Sure we do. We can put it in a ditch, go get the Cliftons' pickup, and tell Ben there's a new plan."

Walter exhaled. He understood Larkin's frustration, but loading up all the medicine in one vehicle made the most sense. They could drive it straight into the Jacobson's barn and secure it without trouble. If the worst happened and the farm was compromised, someone could hop in the driver's seat and get away with the medicine before it was taken.

"Ben's plan is a good one. We just need to take our time and we'll get there."

"Easy for you to say." Larkin's shoulders bunched as the road dipped into a gradual descent. The hospital sat in a small commercial district just above Interstate 80 at the base of the foothills, nearly two thousand feet lower in elevation than the Cliftons' place.

Once they reached Northwoods Boulevard, Walter hoped the truck would gain traction from the better asphalt of a major road. He checked his watch. Just after eight in the morning. Ben expected them by nine. If Larkin kept the truck on the road, they should make it.

Larkin slowed to turn onto Northwoods and the U-Haul slid. Walter reached for the armrest built into the door. The back of the truck kept sliding, twisting the cab in slow motion toward the south and a tall curb.

"Hold on!" Larkin twisted the steering wheel in the opposite direction, trying to angle the front wheels away from the concrete and back onto the road. "I might not save it!"

Walter braced himself. The U-Haul shimmied. The rear tires were spinning, completely tractionless in the melting snow and ice. Walter held his breath. They were going to hit the curb. He didn't think the truck would clear it. If they popped a tire, they would be stranded. Ben would be waiting for hours. Madison, Brianna, and Colt would be vulnerable.

They had to do something. Walter shouted. "Try the brakes!"

"I did!" Larkin cranked the steering wheel back in the other direction and the entire truck shuddered. A rear wheel came off the ground and they tipped toward the west. It wasn't enough.

The U-Haul hit the curb and jumped it one wheel at a time. *Thud, thud.* The back ones followed. *Thud, thud.* The truck's worn-out shocks squealed and the cab bounced up and down before the whole thing came to rest in the front yard of what used to be a ski-themed restaurant.

Larkin shoved the gear shift into park and threw off

his seat belt before stepping out of the cab. He stalked across the snow-dusted weeds and stopped on the edge of the road. Walter gave him a few minutes before getting out and joining him.

"Thanks for not killing us back there."

"We're never going to get this thing back up the mountain."

"Ben's got his F-150 rigged up with some sort of a snowplow, remember? He's going to lead the way. If we can get to the hospital, we can make it to the Jacobson's place."

Larkin pinched the back of his neck. "What if that radio transmission you heard is true? If America is no more and we've got some Unified States thing in its place, what are we going to do?"

"Take it one day at a time, I suppose."

"I'm not risking my life in this truck just for Ben to turn over the medicine to the first guy he sees wearing an official uniform."

"It may never come to that."

Larkin looked over at Walter. "If it does, I'm telling you right now, all deals with the Jacobsons are off."

Walter exhaled. "Understood. Want me to take a turn trying to steer that thing?"

"Knock yourself out."

Two hours later, Walter pulled into the parking lot of the hospital, exhausted from using all his strength to keep the truck on the road. Sweat dripped into his eyes as he backed into a clearing made by Ben's truck at the front doors.

He glanced over at Larkin. "Remind me never to offer to drive again."

The younger man chuckled. "Told you so." He climbed down from the passenger side as Colt and Brianna appeared in the hospital entry.

"About time you two showed up." Colt reached out and gripped Walter's hand before pulling him in for a quick hug. He lowered his voice. "Too much longer and I'd have had to duct tape blondie's mouth shut. She's not exactly a fan of this plan."

"Neither am I." Larkin joined them and Colt leaned over to shake his hand. "I didn't survive this long to die in a U-Haul on the side of the road."

"I told you this was a terrible idea." Brianna stopped a few feet away from the men, hands on her hips. "Ben's lucky you made it when you did. I was ten minutes away from telling him to shove it and loading up the Jeep."

"We still could."

Walter shook his head. "The hard part is over. All we need now is to load up the U-Haul and follow Ben to the farm."

Brianna rolled her eyes. "Have you forgotten how much medicine is back there?"

"The girl has a point." Larkin rolled his shoulders. "I vote for Craig to take the first shift."

"All by himself?"

"Sure beats me doing it." He leaned back against the truck's sidewall, blocking a picture of a Doppler radar forecast. Walter leaned over to read it. "Oklahoma Center for Weather Research, Forecasting & Education."

He shook his head. "Not a lot of jobs for weathermen now."

Colt licked his finger and stuck it in the air. "Forecast for the next two months: cold enough to freeze the balls off a pool table." He jerked his head toward the hospital. "Let's get on with it."

Walter ducked his head and smiled. Even if they disagreed on the best method to secure the medicine, he'd grown to love every member of his new family and was thankful to know them. He followed the men inside where Craig and Ben Jacobson were positioned at the entrance to the pharmacy.

"Our apologies on the delay. Roads were a little slippery."

"Understood." Ben turned toward the fire doors. They were bent off their hinges.

Walter frowned. "Did you break them down to get in?"

"Someone beat us to it." Craig frowned. "When Brianna and I got here, the doors were wide open, but that wasn't the worst of it."

"What was?"

Craig's mouth turned down in a grimace. "Some jerk boobytrapped the pharmacy with a smoke grenade. I about shot my own foot off reaching for my gun."

"Anyone inside?"

"Nope. But whoever it was messed the place up pretty good and cleared most of a shelf."

"What did they take?"

"A little bit of everything. No rhyme or reason to it that we could see."

Walter nodded. "Amateurs. Not someone familiar with medicine."

Larkin chimed in. "Could have been the guy we fought off. He didn't look like a medical professional if you know what I mean."

Ben agreed. "That's what we figure. He got in, grabbed what he could and left behind a parting gift."

"That could mean he's gone for good."

Larkin shook his head. "Or that he's shown his boss the haul and they're planning to take the rest any minute. That guy wouldn't have gone through all the work to get in just to take an armful and leave. He'll be back."

"Then we need to hurry." Walter strode into the pharmacy. His daughter stood in the back, pulling an armful of medicine off a shelf. He hurried over and waited until she dumped the medicine in the box before giving her a hug. "Are you all right?"

Madison nodded. "I'm fine." She pointed to a row of boxes closest to the door. "You can start with those."

Walter smiled. Madison was all business and Walter appreciated it. He stepped over to the first box and picked it up. It was labeled *Acarbose to Dibucaine*. "What's in here?"

"All the drugs that would fit in the box from the first shelf." Madison waved at the rest of the pharmacy. "Everything's alphabetical by generic name."

Walter nodded in understanding before carrying the box past Larkin and Colt, who lined up to take a load.

Without a medical professional like Heather Jacobson or at least a drug index, he wouldn't know what ninety-nine percent of the drugs in the pharmacy even were. He'd be liable to kill someone with the wrong drug before he helped.

It was another reason they needed to keep the alliance with the Jacobsons on good terms. Heather was one of the most useful people around for miles. Maybe even in the entire state.

Craig caught up with him, carrying two boxes stacked on top of each other. "Thanks for driving down here. Larkin said it wasn't easy."

Walter smiled. "You're welcome. Thanks for protecting the pharmacy." He set the box on the truck bed and Brianna picked it up and carried it into the back. Craig did the same and they walked side-by-side back toward the pharmacy. "How's Daniel?"

"Stable. Heather says he's lucky they found him when they did. If Tracy hadn't kept pressure on his wound, he'd have bled out for sure."

"Sorry about John."

Craig nodded and the pair lapsed into silence, carting box after box out to the truck for Brianna to pack away.

The sun hung high in the sky by the time the last box made it into the truck. Walter leaned against the side and chugged a bottle of water. "I'm glad that's over with."

Larkin looked up at the countless stacks of boxes. "Now comes the hard part." He grimaced. "We have to drive it uphill."

CHAPTER TWELVE
WALTER

Access Road
   Truckee Mountain Hospital
   Truckee, CA
   3:00 p.m.

"The F-150 is doing the job." Walter watched the truck in front of them scrape the road free of slush and ice. After some trial and error, Ben and Craig managed to lower the snowplow attached to the front end low enough to scrape most of the ice off the road. It wasn't fast work, but it beat sliding off the road and into a ditch.

Larkin didn't share Walter's enthusiasm. "I'll believe it when we get there in one piece."

Walter exhaled and dipped his head low enough to catch sight of Brianna's canary-yellow Jeep behind them. They were driving like a convoy. Ben and Craig in the lead, U-Haul with Larkin and Walter in the cab in the middle, and Brianna and Madison taking up the rear in the Jeep. Colt sat in the back of the U-Haul, sandwiched between boxes of medicine as a last line of defense.

"Even if we make it to Ben's place, that doesn't mean the medicine is safe." Larkin glanced over at Walter. "We were attacked at the Cliftons' and it's more secluded than the Jacobsons' farm."

"You think we should store it somewhere else?"

Larkin shrugged. "I don't know. But keeping it all in one place doesn't sit well with me. I'd prefer to split it up."

Walter saw the point and the two began brainstorming options for storage. While they talked, Ben's F-150 cleared the road out of the commercial district, and onto Northwoods Boulevard. The U-Haul's engine groaned as they began the ascent up the mountain.

Larkin pressed on the gas and ground his teeth together. "The rear tires are slipping."

"Can you keep it on the road?"

"I sure as hell hope so." He sat straighter in the seat. "Last thing I want to do is unload a bunch of medicine in the middle of a snowbank with this wind."

Walter reached for the armrest and held on as Larkin eased the truck into a curve. As they came out of it, the F-150's brake lights flashed three times as it came to a stop.

"What the—?" Larkin leaned closer to the windshield. "Please tell me that's not what it looks like."

Past Ben's pickup, a collection of short, dark colored vehicles covered the road. Walter squinted. "Looks like snowmobiles."

Larkin cursed. "We're too late."

"What do you mean?"

"The guy who killed John and shot Daniel; he drove a snowmobile."

Walter's heart picked up speed. "There's a lot more than one."

"No shit." Larkin eased his foot off the gas. "What do we do?"

"Hit the brakes a few times to alert Brianna." Walter leaned down to catch sight of his daughter and Brianna in the Jeep. As Larkin tapped the brakes, the Jeep slowed.

Walter turned to look out the windows. Pine trees lined the road as far as Walter could see to his left and right. Past the snowmobiles, he could make out the sign for a small ski hotel that used to serve tourists in the winter. It was too far away to reach. He clenched his fists. "Any way around them?"

Larkin shook his head. "Maybe in the Jeep. But they're blocking the whole road. Even if I punched the gas and somehow made it onto the side, I wouldn't get very far. The trees are too dense and the snow is too thick."

Walter bent down and picked up the rifle off the floorboard. He checked to confirm it was loaded and ready to fire before handing it over to Larkin. "If you back up, can you get enough traction to get up to highway speed?"

"With the road curving like it does back there?" Larkin twisted around to confirm. "I'll be lucky if I make it up to thirty before I tip the whole rig on its side."

"Then we can't ram them." Walter picked up his own rifle and readied it. "We'll have to shoot our way out." He reached for the window crank when Larkin held up a hand.

"Hold on."

Walter glanced up. The door to the F-150 stood open and Craig Jacobson was walking toward the roadblock. A man swung over the closest snowmobile's seat and stood up before pulling off a black helmet. A rush of graying hair sprung up on his head and a thick beard covered his neck.

They were too far away to see much more, but the way he carried himself spoke of a hard life with tough choices. This wasn't the man's first standoff.

"How many are there?"

Walter attempted to count. "Hard to tell since the snowmobiles are all the same color. I'd say at least seven or eight. Maybe more."

"I can't see any weapons, can you?"

"Not clearly. But that doesn't mean they aren't loaded for war. Looks like they're all outfitted in the same gear. Black snowmobile suits and helmets. Could have guns stashed in every pocket."

"Or grenades." Larkin shuddered. "This is bad. Real bad."

Walter watched as Craig closed the distance between the F-150 and the lead snowmobile. He stopped ten feet in front of the only man from the roadblock to leave his rig. Walter cranked down the U-Haul window to try and hear their conversation. He couldn't make out much.

"...get through."

"...missing shipment... check it..."

"What are they talking about?" Larkin cranked his own window and a current of cold wind pushed through the cab.

"I can't tell for sure. Something about a delivery."

"That's bull and everyone knows it. They want what's in the back."

"They aren't going to get it." Walter looked in the rearview. Brianna and Madison still sat in the Jeep, fifty feet or so behind the U-Haul. Steam billowed around the rear of the vehicle and Walter exhaled. If they needed to, the girls could get away.

Craig's voice rose above the idling engine. "No way! Move!"

"Not good." Larkin held the rifle in his lap and reached for a Glock he carried in an appendix holster.

Walter stuck his hand out the window and stuck his thumb down for a moment before bringing it back inside. He hoped Madison and Brianna caught it. They needed to know this was going south and that trouble could break out at any time.

Craig pointed at the road before throwing his arms up in the air. Larkin shifted the U-Haul into reverse.

"What are you doing?"

"Getting ready." He glanced in the rearview. "If

shooting breaks out, we need some distance between us and them."

A horn honked and the heads of the men Walter could see on the snowmobiles turned toward the pickup. Ben Jacobson had slid over to the driver's seat and shut the door. He honked the horn again.

Craig gestured again and shook his head before turning around. A single gunshot pierced the silence. Craig stumbled, one, two steps, before sliding to his knees. He clutched his chest and looked up, eyes pleading with his uncle and God and whoever else was out there to help him.

As the pickup truck's door opened, Craig fell, face-first, onto the road.

"No!" Ben screamed as he rose up out of his seat.

Larkin turned to Walter. "It's now or never."

"Now." Walter braced himself as Larkin punched the gas. The rear tires squealed and the back end shimmied. He hoped Colt had a safe place to hunker down back there.

Larkin steered with one hand as he craned his neck out the window to see behind the trailer. "Cover me!"

Walter propped the rifle on the open window and took aim. The U-Haul skittered back and forth. "Don't hit the Jeep!"

"Don't let me get shot!" Larkin turned the wheel as the U-Haul neared the Jeep.

A volley of shots rang out. Bullets slammed into the F-150 one after the other. Walter took aim. The U-Haul bounced all over the road, swerving left and right as Larkin struggled to maintain control.

"I can't take a shot with you driving like that!"

"You try backing up a fourteen-foot truck down an icy hill for God's sake!"

Walter checked on Brianna's location. "Stop when I say. Five, four, three, two, now!"

Larkin braked and the U-Haul slid to a stop alongside the Jeep. Walter glanced up at the snowmobiles. A hundred and fifty feet was still in range for most anything. They didn't have much time.

Brianna rolled down her window. "What's happening?"

"Craig's been shot. Ben's taking fire."

"What do we do?"

"We're going to keep backing up and see if we can make it all the way to the on-ramp for I-80."

"And then what?"

"Hope it's clear enough to outrun them. Snowmobiles can't drive on a dry road."

Engines revved and Walter jerked his head. "They're coming!"

"What should we do?"

Walter hated what he was about to say with every fiber of his being, but they had to protect the medicine. He made eye contact with his daughter. "Try and give us cover. But as soon as we clear this curve, take off."

Madison leaned over Brianna. "I love you, Dad!"

"Love you too, sweetheart. Stay safe. I'll find you."

Walter motioned to Larkin and he punched the gas. The U-Haul lurched into reverse as Madison propped a rifle on her door ledge. Walter sent up a prayer. If they couldn't outrun the snowmobiles, none of them might make it out of this ambush alive.

CHAPTER THIRTEEN
MADISON

Northwoods Boulevard
  Truckee, CA
  4:00 p.m.

"We're never going to be able to hold them!" Madison fired another shot at the nearest snowmobile. The driver was crouched behind the seat, gun of his own propped on the vinyl. "If we don't get out of here, the Jeep's going to be so shot full of holes, we won't be able to drive it."

Brianna fired a series of shots, taking aim at four men, one after the other. "We have to buy your dad and Larkin enough time to make it to the road." She fired again and a man fell back into the snow. She whooped. "I got one!"

Madison gritted her teeth. Of all the crazy plans they'd thought up over the past year, this had to be one of the worst. The Jeep was a sitting duck out there with its bright yellow paint glinting in the winter sun. Even if they could navigate the snowy woods to their right, any one of the snowmobiles could follow.

"If we make it out of here alive, we're giving this thing a makeover."

"Are not! She's gorgeous."

"We're a target."

"Just means we need to eliminate the threat." Brianna grabbed a full magazine off the seat and changed it out. "I've got two left. How about you?"

"Three." Madison leaned over and took aim. As she fired off another shot, a smattering of bullets hit the Jeep in a wide arc. "What the hell are they firing?"

"A bunch of rifles is my guess."

"They must have endless ammunition."

A round pierced the windshield and lodged in the seat back where Brianna's head would rest. It left an inch-wide hole and concentric splinters in the glass. It would never hold.

"We've got to get out of here!" Madison twisted around in time to catch a snowmobile on the edge of her peripheral vision taking off, gunning for the tree line to Brianna's left side. "On your left!"

Brianna swiveled and fired. She missed.

More shots hit the Jeep and the girls ducked behind the doors. After the shots faded, Madison risked a glance. "It's gaining."

Brianna rose up and fired again. The snow machine kept coming.

"We have to move, Brianna."

"No. I can take him out."

Another snowmobile pulled out from ahead. "There's another one!" There were too many men and not enough cover. They would never survive sitting out on the road. Her heart hammered against her ribs. "We need to go! Now!"

"Where's your dad?"

Madison turned around. "They've cleared the curve."

"What about Ben?"

Madison turned back toward the F-150. Ben was nowhere to be seen. "I can't get a visual. He could already be dead."

"Or he's trapped up there, using all his ammo to keep us alive."

A bullet hit the Jeep's door six inches below Madison's face. "If we stay here, we won't be for much longer." Madison aimed at the snowmobile coming her way in the snowbank. As it rose over a hill of powder, she fired. The driver jerked back, left hand flying off the handlebar.

Hope filled her for a moment, but he shook off the shot and leaned back over. The realization hit her like the bullets pocking the Jeep. "I think they're wearing vests."

"Are you serious?" Brianna cursed and dropped the rifle on the seat. She shoved the Jeep into drive. "Try and cover me."

Madison stuck her rifle out the window and fired a series of shots at the snowmobile gaining the most ground. The driver slowed and ducked as Brianna sprayed an arc of wet snow across the road. The tires slipped on the wet asphalt, but Brianna kept the four-by-four on the road until they reached the shoulder.

"Here we go!" She hit the snow bank and clumps of wet snow and ice flew in all directions. They cleared the worst of the hill and Brianna punched the gas, slipping and sliding all over the place until the thick tires dug into the forest floor beneath the snow.

Madison unhooked her seatbelt and clambered into the back seat with her gun. Two snowmobiles followed them into the trees. She kneeled on the rear seat and unzipped the rear window on the soft top before positioning the rifle in the opening. "I'll keep shooting. Maybe we can slow them down."

"Good. Because I have no idea where I'm going!"

While Brianna kept driving farther into the forest, Madison took aim. The Jeep hit a dip in the ground as she fired and the shot went high. She cursed and tried again. Wide left.

The Jeep slowed and the snowmobiles gained. She shouted back at Brianna. "What's going on?"

"I can't see more than ten or fifteen feet ahead. Too many trees and this busted windshield is giving me fits!"

Damn it. Madison sucked in a breath and tried to focus. She couldn't let them overtake them or run them into a tree. She had to make the shot.

I can do this. She swallowed a thick wad of spit and fear and leaned over to bring the closest driver into her sights. Bulletproof vests meant she couldn't aim for the big, squishy middle and the easy target. She had to shoot to kill.

Madison exhaled and fired a cluster of shots, pulling the trigger five times in a row. The last shot hit the driver in the head. He flew back, landing hard in the snow. The snowmobile kept coming, engine running, driverless. It slammed into a tree and flipped on its side.

The other driver swerved his rig around the crashed snowmobile and accelerated. He couldn't have been more than thirty feet behind them.

Madison called to Brianna. "I got one!"

"Is he dead?"

"I don't think so, but his snowmobile is in a tree."

"What about the other one?"

She grimaced. "Gaining." Madison leaned over and fired another series of shots. The snowmobile jerked and slowed for a moment before darting to the left. "I might have hit him, but he's still coming."

"Shoot him!"

"It's not that easy." Madison twisted to face the driver's side of the Jeep. "He's moved into the trees. He's flanking us on your side."

Brianna turned in the front seat. "I see him!"

Madison unzipped the side window and flecks of snow kicked up from the Jeep's tires pelted her in the face. She leaned over and tried to aim, but the bits of flying snow and ice kept coming. Every time a needle of ice landed near her eye, she blinked. "I can't get a shot. Too much kickback from the tires."

"Could you shoot out the back?"

"Yes."

"I'll speed up and see if we can get ahead of him."

Before Madison could object, Brianna punched the gas. Madison fell onto the floorboard and her rifle clattered down on top of her. As she struggled to right herself, Brianna let out a shout.

"Hold on!"

Madison curled up into a ball as the Jeep lost traction on the passenger side. Two wheels came off the ground. Brianna screamed. The four-by-four slammed into something hard and unforgiving. Forward momentum threw Madison against Brianna's seat and her head slammed into the door.

The entire rear of the vehicle lifted, propelled forward by the Jeep's speed and velocity pre-crash. It hung in the air a moment, a few feet off the ground, before crashing back to earth. Madison bounced against the floorboard. Pain arced across her hip.

The world was still.

"Brianna?" Madison struggled to sit up. "Are you all right?"

Her best friend didn't answer. Madison's head pounded and her eyes couldn't focus. She had to move. The last snowmobile driver was out there. "Brianna?"

Finally, a groan. "I'm here."

"Are you hurt?"

"I think my leg is broken."

Madison pressed her lips together. They would never be able to escape on foot now. She eased up to look out the rear driver's-side window.

"Any sign of the asshole chasing us?"

"Not yet." Madison maneuvered around the back

seat of the Jeep, avoiding the contents that flew about in the crash, to retrieve her rifle. "He's got to be watching us. What is he waiting for?"

"To see if we're still alive is my guess."

"Can you walk?"

Brianna grunted. "Not likely."

"Then I have to flush him out."

"No." Brianna tried to twist in the seat, letting out a shout of pain before falling back. "You'll be dead before you make it five feet."

"We can't just stay in here."

"That's exactly what we do. Eventually, curiosity will get the better of him and he'll expose himself."

"Then what?"

"We shoot him." Brianna groaned and Madison eased through the two front seats. She gasped. Brianna's leg wasn't just broken. Her knee had swollen more than twice its normal size. It looked like a grapefruit sitting on top of her leg.

"You need help. Pain relievers and ice and probably a brace."

"Everything's in the U-Haul." Brianna grunted out the words as she tried to move her leg to elevate it. She made it halfway before letting out a sob. "You have to stay vigilant and find that guy. It's the only way out of here."

"Will the Jeep start?"

Brianna frowned. "I don't know."

"Try it."

She pressed her good foot on the brake and turned the key. It clicked but wouldn't turn over. Brianna tried a few more times, cranking the key and pumping the gas before leaning back in defeat. "Nope."

"Then I'll have to hike out and find the U-Haul." Madison glanced the way they came. "Assuming my dad and Larkin were able to save it."

"Don't forget Colt. He's in the back."

Madison would have given anything to have one of the three men with them right now. She chewed on her lip. "Try to rest. I'll watch for the snowmobile or the driver. If I don't see him soon, I'll head out."

Brianna nodded and Madison climbed back into the back seat. She zipped up the windows to preserve what little heat was left inside the vehicle before fishing a pair of binoculars out of the rear cargo area. Starting on the driver's side, Madison worked her way slowly around the Jeep, looking for anything out of the ordinary. Halfway around, she saw something dark in the snow in the direction the snowmobile had been headed. There was too much uneven ground and too many trees to be sure.

She glanced up at the sky. Nightfall would be coming soon. If she didn't find the man before it got dark, Madison didn't know what she was going to do.

After watching for thirty minutes, she leaned over to check on Brianna. Her best friend leaned back against the driver's seat, eyes closed. Madison shook her shoulder. "Brianna?"

No response.

She shook her a little harder and her head lolled to the side. *Crap.* She thought back to the crash and pulled Brianna's hair away from her face. A goose egg the size of her fist swelled on the side of the head to match her knee. Brianna must have slammed into the steering wheel. She probably had a concussion.

Madison shivered. The temperature in the Jeep was rapidly dropping. If she didn't figure out a way to keep Brianna warm, she would freeze to death.

CHAPTER FOURTEEN

WALTER

Northwoods Boulevard
 Truckee, CA
 5:00 p.m.

Larkin slowed the U-Haul to a stop and turned back to face the front.

Walter let out a trapped breath. "They aren't coming."

"Not yet."

"We should go back for Ben."

"He's probably already dead."

"You don't know that."

Larkin checked the gauges on the truck. "If this were summer, we'd be an overheated mess right now."

"If this were summer, we wouldn't be in a face-off with a pack of snowmobiles."

"Guess that's one good thing about the snow." Larkin

leaned back and rubbed a hand down his face. "Did you see what happened to Brianna and Madison?"

"I saw the Jeep take off for the woods right before we turned the corner."

"Anyone follow them?"

"I couldn't see." Walter looked toward the tree line where Brianna had driven. "But I would have if I were them." He hoped his daughter and her best friend either shot the men who followed them or got away. "If they die because of this…"

"Don't think like that."

"I can't help it." Walter slammed his fist on the dash and opened up the passenger-side door.

"What are you doing?"

"Going to help Ben. I can't leave him all alone."

"You might as well shoot yourself in the head right now and be done with it."

Walter frowned. "I'm not sitting here waiting for them to chase us."

"I'm down to my last magazine. You?"

"One full and one partial."

Larkin groaned and opened the door. "Just for the record, this is stupid."

Walter smiled. "Noted. I'll tell Colt." He stepped down from the cab of the U-Haul as the sound of an engine and tires slipping on snow stopped him. The F-150 careened into view, riddled with bullet holes and sliding all over the road. Ben sat behind the wheel, blood coating his face.

Larkin honked the horn and Ben slowed the truck to

a stop beside Walter. He collapsed against the steering wheel and Walter rushed to his side.

The driver's door was pocked with half a dozen holes and as Walter yanked it open, blood dripped off the floorboard and onto his shoe. He called out to Larkin. "He's been shot. More than once."

"How many?"

Walter grimaced. "Too many." He slung his rifle over his shoulder and stepped up into the truck. "Help me get him back to Colt."

He grabbed the bigger man beneath the arm and dragged him out. Larkin hurried to help and together they pulled Ben Jacobson from the driver's seat and down to the snow. Two holes punctured his ski jacket and blood coated his right leg.

"Could be three or more." Larkin's tone was grim. "He'll never make it."

"We have to try. Help me carry him."

They worked as a team, Walter carrying Ben's upper body and Larkin his lower, all the way past the U-Haul to the rear door. Walter braced Ben's body against his chest before banging on the roll-up door in a three-two-three pattern. He waited five seconds and cranked it open.

The barrel of Colt's Sig Sauer greeted him, followed by Colt's anxious face. He paled when he saw Ben's body. "Guess I don't have to ask what happened."

"Snowmobiles. A lot of them. Don't know how many are left." Walter grunted and hoisted Ben higher. "Help us get him inside."

With Colt's added strength, the three men lifted Ben

into the back of the U-Haul and laid him out. Walter stepped back and wiped the blood off his hands. "I've got to get back out there."

"Let me go." Colt stood and stepped around Ben. "I've been cooped up back here while you all have done the fighting."

Larkin nodded. "He's right. They won't be expecting him."

Walter hesitated. He wanted to be the one to find his daughter. "Madison and Brianna took off in the Jeep. They might have snowmobiles in pursuit."

"Why haven't they followed us here?"

"Too dry. Ben's snowplow did a good enough job on the road. Back up the road where the forest begins, there's plenty of room to off-road, but down here it's too tight or the ground is too dry."

Colt nodded. "I'll come at them from the side. Try and circle around and take out anyone who's left."

"I'll come with you." Larkin looped his rifle over his shoulder and pulled out his handgun. "Together we should be able to flush them out."

Walter glanced at Ben. "I'll see what I can do here."

Colt clapped him on the back. "If we don't come back in an hour, assume the worst."

"You're coming back." Walter nodded at Larkin. "I need him to drive this tin can home."

Colt and Larkin hopped down and pulled the U-Haul door shut behind them. Walter turned his attention to Ben Jacobson. He crouched beside the large man and rested his hands on his thighs. "We're going to fix you up and you're going to pull through this and I don't want to hear anything to the contrary."

Walter stood up and turned to face the boxes. He couldn't just open up Ben's jacket without supplies. He scanned the names, looking for anything familiar. After what seemed like forever, he found packets of QuikClot, gauze, and bandages.

He wasn't as good as Heather at dealing with gunshot wounds, but he could manage as long they weren't too bad. Walter had kept Drew alive through their escape from Sacramento despite a bullet and no antibiotics. Saving Ben in the back of a U-Haul couldn't be worse than that.

After laying everything beside him, Walter leaned over and found the zipper to Ben's jacket and pulled it down before pushing the thick down insulation aside. Blood coated Ben's sweater, turning the light gray wool deep red.

Walter pulled off his own jacket and pushed up his sleeves before tugging a small multitool from his pocket. He flicked open the knife and used it to cut away Ben's sweater and shirt.

Just as he'd feared, two bullet wounds marred Ben's torso. One barely an inch in from his side and one through his upper shoulder. Walter hated to roll the man, but he had no choice. With gentle pressure, he rolled Ben first one way and then another before laying him back down in relief.

Both bullets were through-and-through. Judging by the size of the exit wounds, he was looking at high-velocity military ammunition. M-4s excelled as long range weapons, but caused problems of collateral damage up close. An on-target round fired from a military rifle could take out the intended target and someone standing a ways behind.

Walter grabbed a bottle of alcohol he found and poured a generous amount over both the entry and exit of the first wound. As the drying blood washed away, fresh blood oozed from the wound. He needed to stop the bleeding before Ben lost too much more or nothing he did afterward would matter.

Walter reached for two QuikClot packs and ripped them open, positioning them on the wounds. Using the bandage, he wrapped Ben's middle, holding the QuikClot in place before securing it with butterfly clips. It wouldn't be permanent, but it might get him home alive.

After the abdominal wound was secure, Walter repeated the steps with the shoulder wound, wrapping the clotting packs in the bandage and securing it tight. He leaned back on his heels and wiped at the sweat dripping down his nose before turning to Ben's legs.

Apart from some bruising developing across his thigh, Ben's legs were fine. The blood covering his pant leg must have come from the abdominal through and through. *Thank God for small favors.* Walter cleaned up the mess as best he could and zipped Ben's jacket back up to keep the man warm.

He thought about what else he could do. An IV was out of the question in the U-Haul, as were any oral form of antibiotic or fluids. Until Larkin and Colt came back, there wasn't anything to do but wait.

After a quick drink of water, Walter eased up against the side of the U-Haul and reached for Ben's hand.

"Ben, can you hear me?" Walter checked for a pulse. Slow, but steady. "It's Walter Sloane. You've been shot, but you're going to be all right." Walter waited for a response. When none came, he kept talking, mentioning Jenny and Ben's kids and telling him how important it was that he pulled through. Halfway through a story about Lilly and a runaway chicken, Ben groaned.

"I feel like I've been hit by a truck."

Walter smiled in relief. "Worse. You've been shot. Twice."

"You're right. That is worse." Ben tried to laugh but he grunted in pain instead. "How bad is it?"

"If we can get you back to Heather, you should pull through."

"No, I mean the ambush. Are we all that's left?"

Walter shook his head and explained what happened from his point of view.

Ben moaned. "I never should have kept the medicine at the pharmacy. We should have moved it in small batches over the course of the summer."

"You did what you thought was best at the time."

"No I didn't." Ben coughed and reached for his side, but Walter caught his hand.

"Careful." He grabbed a bottle of water and a medicine cup and poured enough in for Ben to swallow a mouthful.

"Thanks." Ben took a few deep breaths before continuing. "I told everyone from the beginning that all we had to do was hold out for the government. Sooner or later FEMA or the military or someone would be coming. It was my way to keep everyone positive and keep it all together." He coughed again. "It was stupid."

"We've all done things that in hindsight we wished we hadn't done. When I think back to the EMP..." Walter shook his head. "I never should have gotten on that airplane. I should have stayed home and put my family first."

"You didn't know what would happen."

Walter exhaled. Truth was, he'd been warned by the space weather reports and by his wife. He should have followed his gut then and every day thereafter. Right now, his gut told him Ben Jacobson could be more than an ally. He could be a friend.

He squeezed the man's hand. "Rest now. We'll get you home soon."

Ben slipped off to sleep. A few minutes later, the U-Haul door creaked.

Walter reached for his gun.

CHAPTER FIFTEEN
WALTER

Northwoods Boulevard
  Truckee, CA
  6:oo p.m.

The door to the U-Haul cranked open, revealing Colt's stocky legs and grim expression. He dumped an armful of rifles and shotguns on the floor and spat on the ground. "All clear. We're now the proud owners of five snowmobiles, four rifles, two shotguns, two revolvers, one Glock, and five dead bodies."

Larkin rounded the corner of the trailer, carrying a bag too full to close. "Add in a crap ton of magazines and ammo, too. These guys weren't messing around."

Walter shook his head. "We're lucky to be alive."

Colt motioned to Ben. "How's he?"

"Breathing. He was awake for a few minutes while I

patched him up. Two through-and-throughs. If we can get him somewhere comfortable, he should survive, assuming there's no internal damage."

"Then we should head out before any more of these assholes show up."

"Not without Madison and Brianna."

Colt glanced behind him with a frown. "They're probably back at the Cliftons' place by now."

Walter wasn't convinced. "Did you see their tracks? Any evidence they were followed?"

Larkin scratched his beard. "It's hard to tell now that the sun's gone down, but I might have found where they turned off the road. Looks like at least one snowmobile followed them, if not two."

"I'm not leaving here until I know for sure." Walter stood up and stretched his aching muscles. His entire backside was numb from the cold metal of the trailer. "You two should take the U-Haul and Ben straight to Heather. She'll know what to do."

Colt glanced at Larkin. "I'm not taking Ben home without you. We can take him to the Cliftons' place, but I'm not stepping foot on the Jacobson farm with him in this condition."

"What?" Walter shook his head. "That makes no sense. Jenny will be worried sick."

"We pull up there in the U-Haul, just me and Larkin, and they're liable to shoot us on sight. They'll blame us for Craig's death and Ben's injuries. It'll be a nightmare."

"That's nonsense. They'll be thankful he's alive and that you brought the medicine."

Colt tugged on his shirt collar. "That's the other thing. I don't think we should deliver the medicine to them. It needs to be kept somewhere safe where it won't be handed over to the government first thing."

Walter couldn't believe what he was hearing. It was basically a coup. He turned to Larkin. "Do you agree with him?"

"After seeing them almost kill Dani, unfortunately I do. If you were coming with us, we might be able to convince them, but they hate Colt and I'm not their favorite. First I show up with Daniel all shot to hell, then I tell them John is dead. If I bring Ben in unconscious and on death's door, I'll never make it out of there in one piece."

Colt nodded his head in agreement. "Keeping the medicine gives us a bargaining chip. If Ben dies, we'll have something to negotiate."

Walter palmed his forehead and looked down at Ben Jacobson. He couldn't believe the words out of Colt and Larkin's mouths. The past two weeks had given him hope they could form a real alliance and work together to make something lasting. But staring at Ben brought it all full circle.

Madison was out there somewhere and Walter needed to find her. The reality of living on the edge of survival meant family came first. Even if they could somehow mend the fences Colt and Larkin were about to break, none of it would matter if Walter couldn't keep his family safe.

He reached down and picked up his own rifle before motioning to Larkin's bag. "Anything in there I can use?"

"Plenty." Larkin fished out a box of ammunition and another magazine and handed both over. "You sure you want to stay?"

Walter nodded. "I have to find them."

"You should take the F-150. We'll take the U-Haul."

"A truck won't do me much good out in the forest. Do any of the snowmobiles still run?"

"Do you know how to ride?"

Walter shrugged. "Guess I'm about to find out."

Colt suppressed a smile. "Find one that's still warm. Then you won't have to use the choke."

"Anything else I should know?"

"It's like riding a bobcat with skis. The back has a caterpillar, the front two ski blades. As long as you stick to compacted snow, you should be fine."

"And if I don't?"

"Then you probably won't get very far."

Walter nodded. "I'll keep that in mind. Good luck to both of you."

"We'll need it." Colt climbed up into the U-Haul as Walter walked up the road toward the snowmobiles.

All five vehicles were clustered together on the side of the road thanks to Colt and Larkin. Walter put his hand on the hood of each engine and selected the warmest one. He straddled the seat and pulled on his gloves and sunglasses before zipping up his coat.

He might not be experienced in snowmobiling, but he'd skied a few times in his life and he knew how cold the wind could be. The keys sat in the ignition and Walter looked around for a gas pedal. Nothing. He focused on the handlebars and found what looked to be gas on the left and a brake on the right.

Not that different than a motorcycle. He looked behind him at the caterpillar tread and then up front at the pair of skis. "Here goes nothing." With his left hand, he turned the key and pulled the cord. The engine sputtered to life.

After letting the vehicle warm for a few minutes, Walter stuck his feet on the footwells, grabbed the handlebars, and eased on the gas. It didn't move. He frowned and tried again, tightening his grip on the gas. The snowmobile shot forward, kicking snow behind him in an arc. Walter let up and it stopped.

Okay. Really different than a motorcycle. Walter gave himself a pep talk about flying 747s across the ocean and tried again. The snowmobile eased forward and Walter leaned into it, taking it up to barely above a jog.

The snow on the side of the road was relatively compact and he followed what looked to be other tracks slowly toward the tree line. The single headlight illuminated the snow in front of him enough to follow the tracks when they joined a disturbance in the snow. More tracks joined and diverged at the edge of the woods, but Walter couldn't tell which ones were made by Brianna's Jeep or the snowmobiles.

He shook his head. Whoever made the tracks didn't matter. He was following a path and at some point Walter would either find his daughter or find the men who ambushed them on the road. Either way, he made the right choice.

The snow deepened the farther he drove into the forest and every time the tracks curved, he slowed to keep from tipping the snowmobile. His progress slowed to a few miles an hour.

The trees closed in and Walter grew wary. Could the Jeep even fit through a space this tight? His visibility declined the denser the forest grew and Walter narrowly missed sideswiping a fallen pine. The sky darkened even more and he needed the single headlight to see anything. It slowed him even more.

I'm taking too long.

The temperatures were rapidly dropping and without a helmet, his ears and face were freezing. If he didn't find Madison soon, he'd risk frostbite and hypothermia. Without a vehicle to hunker down inside, he wouldn't be able to keep himself warm. For the first time, Walter regretted hopping on the snowmobile without a real plan, but it was short-lived.

Madison needed him. There was no turning back.

As the ruts in the snow curved to the left, Walter leaned and followed. They opened up into a clearing and he squeezed the gas. The snowmobile shot forward. Finally, he could cover some ground. The snowmobile flew across the snowy field and Walter edged it faster.

He didn't see the hump in the snow until it was too late. Straight ahead, something was buried. The headlight flashed against the black fiberglass and Walter jerked the handlebars.

The sled rolled up onto one ski. Walter jerked the other direction. The single ski contacting the snow slipped and Walter lost control. The back twisted out from under him, and the front of the sled flew up and tossed Walter off the back. He landed hard in a bank of melted and refrozen snow. Pain radiated across his lower back. His face burned from the ice and wind.

He lay there for a moment, catching his breath. The single headlight of his wrecked snowmobile shone into the forest twenty feet away. He rolled over and fished out his flashlight before hauling his bruised body up to stand.

Even from that distance he could see the snowmobile was a goner. One of the skis was bent in half. It wouldn't drive again. He turned toward the lump in the snow, easing up to it with the flashlight in one hand and his other inside his pocket, ready to pull out a pistol.

He shined the flashlight on the housing. Another snowmobile. He spun around in a circle and found a boot sticking out of the snow about ten feet away.

The man was sprawled out, half his face a bloody mess. Walter bent to check for a pulse. Practically frozen. He probably died before his body hit the ground.

Walter shivered. That wouldn't happen to him or his daughter. Walter rooted around the body, found another handgun, and shoved it in his ski pants pocket before turning back toward the track. On foot, he could make out the deeper marks of tire tracks.

Brianna's Jeep.

Weaving in and out of the pair of tracks was a set of

three shallower tracks, one similar to a tire and two straight and even. *A snowmobile.*

Walter steeled himself. The girls were being chased. At first by two snowmobiles, then only one. He clenched his fist and started jogging down the middle of the most compacted track. *Hold on, Madison. I'm coming.*

CHAPTER SIXTEEN

SILAS

Woods north of Truckee, CA
6:00 p.m.

Silas came to with a pounding headache and no feeling in his legs. At first he thought the crash severed his spinal column and he'd lie there, paralyzed, until death finally took him. But after a few minutes, his brain began to function.

He thumped on his leg. Stone cold. He leaned forward with a grunt, tipping his whole upper body over until he found purchase in compacted snow. Using his arms as braces, he shimmied back and forth, working his lower body out of the snow. Every twist brought a surge of icy pain shooting in needles down his thighs and calves, all the way to his toes.

Judging by the rapidly diminishing light, he'd been

unconscious for at least half an hour. Plenty of time for his lower body to suffer frostbite. At last, he managed to free his legs, not that it did much good. Silas tried to stand, propping one foot on the snow and dragging his body up using the nearest tree.

He collapsed and ate a mouthful of ice, cursing as he spit it out.

Chasing those girls had been a mistake. Just like everything else that happened that afternoon. He couldn't believe their luck when they first spotted the U-Haul and the productive little worker bees trundling box after box into the back end. The idiots guarding the pharmacy were finally good for something: doing Silas's work for him.

When his uncle heard the good news, he'd clapped Silas on the back and forgiven him then and there for Beckett's death. For a moment, Silas felt the first stirrings of pride. But they'd been extinguished with Elias's next announcement.

A roadblock? They couldn't just swoop in there, guns blazing and take them all out at the hospital? Efficiency wasn't his uncle's style. Not when they could make a show of it for everyone to remember.

But Silas had kept that opinion to himself, dutifully loading up his Polaris and following his uncle through the backwoods trails up to Northwoods Boulevard. No one had anticipated the F-150 with the snowplow attachment. Ingenious, if you asked him. If those pansy-ass guards had some balls and charged the snowmobile line with the truck, it would have been over quicker.

Instead, they chose the hard way: a gunfight. They might as well have been back at the freakin' O.K. Corral in the middle of a shoot-out. One after the other, his cousins went down. Silas almost took a bullet to the head. He was ten seconds away from cutting out to save his own skin when the Big Bird took off for the woods.

Silas and his cousin Aaron followed. That kid had never been good on a pair of skis. When he went down, Silas managed to swerve around him, but watching Aaron's sled slam into a tree threw his concentration. He didn't see the rifle until the bullet hit his thigh.

Everything after that happened too fast to remember. Now he sat in the snow, ass half frozen, with a bullet in his leg and an upside down snowmobile beside him. He didn't know if it would start, but what choice did he have? Unless some fairy godmother floated down from the heavens with a blanket and a flask of whiskey, he needed to get home.

Silas dragged his body over to the snowmobile. The front half was buried in about two feet of snow that had melted from the heat of the engine and then refrozen into ice. There was no way to dig it out without a pickax and Silas didn't have the strength. He clawed through the softer snow using his gloved hands until he found the ignition. He turned the key.

Reaching, he stretched to try and find the choke. It was buried on the other side under even more snow. There was no way for him to reach it without climbing over the sled or crawling all the way around. He tried to stand again and fell, landing hard in the snow on his good leg.

Shit. He couldn't manage anything with an untreated gunshot wound. If the cold didn't kill him, bleeding out would. Gritting his teeth against the pain, he fumbled in the snow for the snowmobile's saddlebags. As he found a buckle and unlatched it, a myriad of contents tumbled out. Extra gloves. A box of ammo. Cigarettes and a lighter. Finally the two things he needed most of all. A handkerchief and small roll of duct tape.

It wouldn't be the greatest tourniquet, but it was all he had. With a grunt, he propped himself up against the snowmobile's side and ripped a wider hole in his pants. The wound stopped bleeding a while ago, more from the cold than any sort of healing. The second he warmed up or tried to walk, it would ooze all over again.

He felt around his thigh for an exit wound.

None. Just my luck.

That meant the bullet was still lodged in his leg. It would have to come out, but not here. All he could do until he reached somewhere warm and secure was wrap it up tight and give his leg some support. He would need it for the road ahead.

Silas ground his teeth against the pain, holding the handkerchief tight against the wound with one hand while he wrapped the duct tape around his leg with the other. After four trips around his thigh, he ripped the last six inches of tape off and used it to seal his pants as best he could.

Night set in fast. He couldn't see more than a foot in

front of his face and even that much was fuzzy and indistinct. Using the snowmobile for support, he hobbled around to the other side before digging out the choke. He flipped it up and gave the cord a pull. Nothing.

He tried five more times, using so much force on the last pull the cord broke. Silas landed in the snow and the pain radiating from his wound stole his breath. He smacked his face. *Get it together*.

With shaking fingers, he reached for the other saddlebag and fished out the two-way radio they used for communication short-range. He tried channel two. "Silas to Cunninghams. Can you read me? Over."

He waited, listening to the static for a minute before trying again. "This is Silas, is anyone out there? Can you guys hear me?"

No response. Either he was out of range or everyone who took part in the ambush was dead. He assumed it was the latter. Out of ideas, Silas stuck his hand in his pocket and fished out a baggie of venison jerky. He chewed the tough meat slowly, using handfuls of snow to wash it down. When it was gone, he leaned back and closed his eyes.

Visions of his father swam in the darkness. Butch Cunningham would be turning in his grave right now if he saw his kid giving up. Once, when Silas was about eight, his dad walked him down to the thrift store and let him pick anything he wanted for ten dollars. Silas chose a bike.

He'd never ridden one before and his old man asked

if he was ready to learn. Silas nodded enthusiastically. "Yes, sir. I'm ready."

Three hours later, two scraped knees and a bloody nose proved otherwise. "I'm just no good at bike ridin'. That's what it is." Eight-year-old Silas wiped the snot from his nose with the back of his hand.

"Is that so?"

"Yes, sir."

His father looked at the bike and then looked at him. "I thought you told me you was ready to learn?"

"I guess I was wrong."

"Are you saying you quit?"

Silas kicked at the dirt. "Maybe."

"Well, no Cunningham gets the luxury of quitting. Come here." His father held the bike and Silas walked toward it. "Get on."

Silas climbed on and held the handlebars.

"I'm going to push you, and you're going to go."

"What if I fall?"

"Then you wipe off the dirt, get up, and do it again."

"How long?"

"Until you can ride."

Silas missed dinner that night. By the time he figured out how to ride a bike, the rooster down the street was crowing his scrawny little head off and Silas was covered in scrapes and bruises. He never asked his father for anything after that.

He never gave up, either.

"First time for everything, old man." Silas reached into his pocket and fished out the cigarettes and the lighter. He lit the end and sucked a puff into his lungs. As the nicotine flooded his brain he squinted into the dark.

"What the…"

He held up the lighter and flicked it. Something shimmered in the distance. He waved the light; it waved back. It was the side mirror to a car.

CHAPTER SEVENTEEN

MADISON

Woods north of Truckee, CA
6:00 p.m.

Her teeth wouldn't stop chattering. Madison tucked the spare coat around Brianna's feet before unfolding an ultra-thin mylar emergency blanket. It felt like metallic tissue paper and tore almost as easily, but it might be enough to keep hypothermia at bay for one of them at least.

Before most trips, Brianna ensured the Jeep was stocked with a small supply of essentials including several MREs, emergency blankets, and potable water. But this hadn't been an ordinary expedition. When Brianna set off for the Jacobsons' farm, she expected to be gone a few hours, not multiple days.

Thanks to the snowmobile jerks, her day trip turned into a three-day bender of standing guard at the ransacked pharmacy and loading medicine onto the U-Haul. There wasn't much left in the Jeep to use.

Madison climbed into the back and rooted through the tossed-about gear. The MREs were gone. One jerry can still held about a gallon of water, but it was too cold to even think about drinking. There were plenty of medical supplies to deal with cuts and scrapes and typical scavenging injuries. Nothing to treat a swollen knee, broken leg, or concussion.

They had one fire puck and a lighter. If she could find something to make a fire, maybe they would stay warm enough until the morning when she could see to hike out. Madison glanced at the rearview window. The world was black. It might as well have been a total canvas cover with no clear plastic at all.

She chewed on her lip, worrying about the last snowmobile driver. Why hadn't he attacked? If he was out there, surely he would have tried to do something by now. One look at the Jeep and anyone would know it wasn't operational.

Maybe he thought they were already dead. Maybe one of the shots she fired out the back hit its mark. She knew the first man crashed, but did the second one as well? After mulling it over for a few minutes, Madison grabbed the fuel puck and the lighter and climbed out the rear passenger-side door.

Wind whipped against her face and stole her breath. She closed her eyes and fought down the panic. They wouldn't freeze to death. She could start a fire. Madison spun around in a circle. There had to be some dry branches somewhere.

With agonizing slowness, Madison searched the nearby area, too frightened to use a flashlight in case their pursuers were still out searching. After what seemed like an eternity, she collected an armful of dead branches she was able to snap off the closest pine trees and hauled them over to the Jeep. Using her boot-clad feet, she pushed the snow around to make a clearing several feet across.

She stopped and looked around. Back when she was younger, she took a trip with her best friend up to Lake Tahoe in the summer. The days were warm, but the nights were cool and to warm up after a day of swimming, they would duck into a small log shack and create their own hot rock sauna.

A Jeep wasn't a log cabin, but she could do the same thing here. All she needed was a collection of large, substantial stones and a means of carrying them. She hiked around the Jeep and up to the rocky outcrop where the right front tire met its end. Crawling on her hands and knees beneath the front bumper, Madison felt around in the dark for rocks small enough to carry, but large enough to retain heat.

She found three. The rest were bits of gravel or too big to lift. It wouldn't be enough. Frustrated, she turned to face the wind and almost shouted for the man on the snowmobile to come and get them. At least then she could shoot him and maybe use his vehicle to find help.

She gave herself a mini pity party before sucking

back her tears and wiping her face. Giving up wouldn't save her or Brianna. After collecting the rocks, she brought them over to the clearing. *Three are better than none.* She set them on the ground, broke the branches into foot-long pieces, and constructed a tepee over the fuel puck.

She fished the lighter from her pocket and flicked the wheel. It didn't start. She tried again. Sparks, but no flame. *Come on.* Madison shook the lighter. The faint sound of butane sloshing around gave her hope. It wasn't empty. She flicked the wheel again.

A flame.

Bending low, Madison cupped the flame and held it against the fuel puck until it lit. She exhaled in relief as the glow of a small fire spread across the surface of the reddish-orange circle. The pucks were advertised as having a three-hour burn time, but through trial and error Madison and the rest of her group discovered they burned much quicker.

If she couldn't get the fire to stay lit without the puck, she had maybe an hour, not much more. A gust of wind blew and the flames sputtered and hissed. Snow landed on the puck and sent wisps of smoke into her face. She moved to block the wind as best she could, but it swirled in the small space between the Jeep and the trees.

The branches wouldn't catch. She didn't know if they were too wet or not old enough or if the wind was too much to bear, but the puck shrank with every passing minute. Sooner or later, it would burn out.

This isn't working. Madison turned back to the Jeep

and tugged open the closest door. She shoved a rifle and the water out of the way, searching for anything that could burn. Everything was plastic or metal or synthetic. She could create plenty of smoke if she needed to send up a signal or boil the water in the can, but she couldn't sustain the fire.

As she shut the door, the branches above the fire puck collapsed and a shower of sparks pocked the snow. The fire turned to smoke and soot. Madison crouched beside the remnants and flicked the lighter. Holding it against the scraps of wood, she willed something to light.

It was a lost cause. After a minute or two, her thumb was on the edge of burning. She was wasting fuel. Madison released the lighter and the flame blinked out. The afterglow drifted across her field of vision, a fading burst of red and orange.

She reached down and picked up the closest stone. It was warm, but the heat wouldn't last for long. After setting them all in the passenger seat, Madison climbed in and shut the door. The temperatures outside were hovering around freezing. Inside wasn't much better.

"Brianna? Can you hear me?" Madison called out to her best friend. She received no response.

She reached over and felt for Brianna's pulse. Steady and strong. Thank God for small favors. One at a time, she tucked the warm stones around her friend's body, placing one at her feet and two on the seat near her hands and chest.

"Don't worry. We're going to make it." Madison climbed into the back and hoisted up the rifle she'd used earlier to shoot at the snowmobiles. As she turned to climb back into the front, something in the distance caught her eye.

She crept closer to the window, squinting into the gloom. *Am I hallucinating already*? She cupped her hands around her face and blocked out everything except the darkness where she'd seen it.

There! Madison dropped her hands and a shiver racked her body. This time, it wasn't from the cold.

Out in the distance, a speck of a light wobbled and glowed. Was it a flashlight? A fire? She couldn't tell from the distance.

She swallowed and checked the status of the rifle. If the light belonged to one of the snowmobile riders, then he was out there, searching. Madison pulled off the glove on her right hand and slipped her finger around the rifle's trigger. Her hand was so cold, she didn't know where the metal began and her skin ended.

Her teeth chattered and her knees knocked together as she stared out the window at the light. It wavered every so often, but it barely moved. Was he hunkered down in the wind? Taking a break?

Madison clamped her teeth to slow the shiver and brought the rifle up into position. She balanced it on the seat back and hunkered down, barely taller than the rear gate of the Jeep, and waited.

No one was sneaking up on them. She would defend herself and Brianna no matter what.

CHAPTER EIGHTEEN

TRACY

Clifton Compound
10:00 p.m.

Tracy sat at the small table, following the wood grain with her fingers. Something was wrong. Even if the loading of the U-Haul took all day, Walter, Madison, and the rest of Tracy's makeshift family should have been home by now.

Fireball purred in her lap, oblivious to her inner turmoil. He'd taken quite a liking to the inside of the cabin over the winter months, refusing to go outside unless someone picked him up and plopped him on the porch. Even then, he'd only rush out to do his business and run back, meowing and clawing to come inside.

She absentmindedly ran her fingers through his fur. "Come spring, you need to earn your keep. More mousing, less snoozing."

At the door, Lottie pricked her ears. The little Yorkie rose up, whole body at attention.

"Are they home?" Tracy stood up and Fireball jumped to the floor.

Lottie whined and pawed at the wood.

"It's okay. I'm coming." Tracy tugged on her coat and yanked the door open. Lottie ran out to the porch barking and jumping. A large pickup truck pulled through the gate to the Cliftons' property, followed by the U-Haul they had prepped early that morning.

Tracy frowned. *This isn't the plan.* She craned her neck to see around the trailer. Where was the Jeep? Tracy bit the inside of her cheek to keep from panicking. *There has to be an explanation. Don't think the worst.*

She stepped off the porch and hurried to meet the pickup truck as the driver's door opened.

"What's happened?"

Colt stepped down. "You know that worst-case scenario we outlined?"

Tracy nodded.

"Think worse." He opened the door to the back seat. "Help me get Ben inside. He needs medical attention."

"Ben Jacobson?" Tracy rushed to the rear of the truck. Ben sprawled across the back seat, one leg dangling down to the floorboard. "Why did you bring him here?"

"It's a long story." Larkin hustled over from the U-Haul. "We can fill you in once he's stable."

Tracy looked past him. "Where's everyone else?"

"Not coming." Larkin reached past her to help Colt

lift Ben from the truck. "We need antibiotics, disinfectant, gauze, and bandages. Maybe sutures."

"We don't have any."

He jerked his head toward the U-Haul. "We have everything."

Tracy swallowed. If they brought all the medicine and Ben here, something awful must have happened. She couldn't go on unless she knew. "Are they dead?"

"What?"

"My husband and my daughter. Are they dead?"

Colt shook his head. "We don't know. Brianna and Madison took off through the woods. A couple of guys followed them. Walter stayed behind to find them."

She swallowed down the horror. "You were attacked."

Colt snapped. "We don't have time, Tracy." He shoved past her, his arms looped under Ben's while Larkin followed with the heavy man's feet. "Help us with Ben or get out of the way."

She stood in the snow, unable to process what was happening. Her husband and daughter were missing, possibly dead, and Colt and Larkin left them behind to save Ben Jacobson. A man whose family was responsible for Dani's almost fatal injury and possibly Walter's as well.

Up until that moment, Tracy had managed to bury her ill feelings toward the Jacobsons, focusing on the positives an alliance could bring. But seeing members of her own little group choose Ben over family? Anger and frustration welled up inside her.

I should have been there. She cursed herself for not insisting on being part of the mission. Now her husband and daughter were out there somewhere and she was supposed to ignore it and focus on a near stranger.

The door to Anne and Barry's cabin opened and Barry stepped out onto the porch, shotgun in his hand.

Anne followed a step behind, jacket flying open in the wind. "What on earth?"

Tracy crossed the common area. "They were attacked. I don't know the details."

"Where's Brianna?"

"Not here. Walter is still out there, searching for the girls."

Barry cursed. "I knew this was a terrible idea."

Anne reached for his arm. "We don't know what's happened. Let's reserve judgment."

"Colt and Larkin brought Ben here. He's wounded."

"What?" Barry bellowed the word. "Why not take him to his own damn farm? They're the ones with all the medicine!"

Tracy pointed to the U-Haul. "They brought the pharmacy, too."

Barry stilled. "Well, at least that's something." He turned to Anne. "Help as best you can. Once Jacobson is stable, we can all sit down and find out what happened."

Anne smiled at Tracy. "Help me treat him, will you? The sooner we deal with it, the sooner we can figure out how to help our daughters."

Tracy exhaled. Anne was right. "I'll root through the

U-Haul for antibiotics, suture kits, and anything else we might need."

"Thank you." Anne strode toward the kitchen cabin where Colt and Larkin had taken Ben.

Tracy hurried to the U-Haul. She yanked the rolling door open and gasped. It was fully loaded almost floor-to-ceiling with box after box of medicine. Her daughter's neat handwriting adorned every box, listing the range of drugs inside. Tracy bit back a sob. She couldn't break down. Not now.

Thanks to the labels, she found the gauze and a suture kit right away. But antibiotics posed a problem. She didn't know the generic names for most shelf-stable versions and searching in penicillin and amoxicillin came up empty. She finally found a box of Zithromax in the Z box, scooped up the rest of the supplies, and hopped out of the truck. She dragged the door shut and ran to the kitchen cabin.

Anne sat in a chair beside a cot, cleaning what looked to be a nasty bullet wound in Ben Jacobson's abdomen. "Sorry that took me so long. I couldn't find any antibiotics."

"There have to be some in there."

Tracy held up a bottle. "These should work, assuming he's not allergic."

"It's a risk we'll have to take. He'll get an infection for sure without them." Anne dipped a clean cotton ball in a small bowl of rubbing alcohol and patted the edges of the wound. "Rifle rounds, both clean with minimal yaw. Lucky for him, they were fired at relatively close range. If he'd been any farther out, we'd be digging bits and pieces from his guts."

"No, we'd be digging a hole in the frozen dirt out back." Colt wiped his hands on a rag and pulled out a chair. He fell into it and closed his eyes.

Larkin sat across from him, a bottle of whiskey and four glasses sitting on the table. While Tracy had been in the U-Haul, both Peyton and Dani had joined the group. Dani leaned against the wall, every bit the angry teenager. Peyton sat on the other side of Ben, helping Anne as best he could.

Tracy turned to the men at the table. "Now that he's being treated, can one of you please tell us what happened?"

Colt tapped the table and Larkin poured a finger of whiskey into a clean glass. Colt downed it, wincing as it hit the back of his throat. "That's bottom of the barrel isn't it?"

"Beggars can't be choosers."

He flashed Larkin the middle finger and turned to Tracy. "They were waiting for us up Northwoods Boulevard. A roadblock of snowmobiles. Looked to be the same type of men as you described."

Larkin nodded. "They were all wearing helmets or glasses and ski masks, so I couldn't get a good look, but they fit the profile."

Tracy exhaled. She'd feared something like that would happen. It was why she and Larkin insisted on moving the drugs, only they were too late.

"Craig got out of the truck to talk to them." Larkin

paused and pressed his fingers against his lips. "They shot him in the back."

Tracy sat up with a start. "What?"

"Immediately after, the bullets started flying. Ben was up in the truck, firing from the open door. Walter and I were in the U-Haul. Brianna and Madison were behind us. There was no way to fight them off. Had to be seven or eight of them, all firing."

He swallowed. "I jammed the U-Haul in reverse and took off back down the road, passed the Jeep, and told them to take off if they couldn't hold. A few minutes later, they did. Walter saw the girls turn for the forest."

"And the men on snowmobiles?"

Larkin exhaled. "Maybe one or two followed them."

Colt joined in. "We took out the rest. By the time the fighting ended, Ben had been hit twice, Craig was dead. We knew at least one snowmobile got away."

"So you left?"

"We had to secure the medicine."

Tracy glanced over at Anne. She didn't look up from Ben's wounds. Tracy shook her head. "Did Walter know where the girls had gone?"

"No. He took a snowmobile and headed into the forest. He planned to follow the tracks."

Tracy closed her eyes. Her husband didn't know the first thing about riding a snowmobile.

"Given the circumstances, we couldn't take Ben home. One look at the two of us dragging him in wounded and we'd probably have been shot."

Colt nodded. "And now we have control of the medicine. If Ben doesn't pull through this, it's all ours."

Anne leaned back in her chair. "They'll see it as an act of betrayal."

"Not if we spin it right."

Anne shook her head. "You've put us in a terrible position."

"No. The Jacobsons did that when they shot me and Walter." Dani pushed off the wall. "Heather's nice, but this whole thing stinks. You should have dropped him off with Heather and taken the medicine."

Colt shot her a glance. "We're doing our best to save him. With the pharmacy's supplies, there's nothing Heather can do that we can't and we don't have to look over our shoulders every ten seconds."

"Not until they come looking for their leader."

"We'll cross that bridge when we come to it."

"What about Madison and Brianna?" Peyton spoke up for the first time. "We can't leave them out there."

Tracy stood up. "I'm going to look for them."

"You'll need help." Larkin leaned back in his chair. "No one should be on Northwoods alone."

"I'll go." Peyton glanced at Anne. "If that's all right with you."

She nodded. "I'm about done here."

Tracy smiled at Peyton. "Get your bag and plenty of extra ammo. We'll leave as soon as we can." She turned and strode from the cabin, not stopping until she stood on the porch of the sleeping cabin across the way. She sucked in a breath of cold air.

Her husband and daughter were out there somewhere, possibly hurt or dying. If the men from the ambush followed them into the forest, could they fight them off? She let out a sob.

Peyton's voice made her jump. "We'll find them, Mrs. S. Don't worry."

"What if it's too late?"

"Brianna and Madison are the toughest girls I know. If anyone can fight off a thug on a snowmobile, it's them."

Tracy managed a small smile. "Thanks, Peyton."

"Let's just go and get them back." He clapped her on the back and pushed past her to grab his gear. After a moment, Tracy followed him inside.

CHAPTER NINETEEN

TRACY

Woods north of Truckee, CA
10:00 p.m.

Madison jerked awake. *Oh, no.* She lay, slumped over the rifle, drooling onto the freezing back seat. At some point, exhaustion overtook her will to stay awake. The man out there could have killed them. Anyone could have crept up on the Jeep and she would have failed. Why didn't he come for them?

She sat up, breath steaming in front of her face. Pain lanced her fingers as she wiggled them inside her gloves. Her feet were two blocks of ice inside her boots. If she hadn't woken up, she would have slowly frozen to death overnight. *What woke me?* Madison twisted around, groaning as her stiff muscles protested.

The world outside the Jeep sat still. Too cold for birds or other forest animals, too dark to see.

Ahh! All of a sudden, she was blinded. White light filled her vision and Madison blinked over and over. Tears welled in her eyes and she held a hand up to shield her face. The light bounced away, forming a wide circle on the ground outside the Jeep.

A flashlight.

Madison sank down beneath the seat back. Was it the light that woke her up? The noise of someone approaching. She didn't know who or what was out there, but she couldn't let them get the best of her. She had to protect Brianna.

After tugging off one glove, Madison reached for the rifle, but recoiled on contact. It was freezing. *I can't hold it steady*.

She twisted around, panic building inside her chest. Brianna carried a backup handgun tucked into an appendix holster. Madison dove beneath the Mylar blanket and dug it out. A Glock 19, warm from Brianna's body heat.

She popped the magazine out and checked the ammunition. *Full, thank God*. She shoved the mag back in place and cursed as the noise filled the Jeep. Did whoever was out there hear her? Did they know the sound?

She didn't know what to do. Staying inside meant limited lines of sight and overwhelming fear. Every bump, every sound, every flash of light would drive terror into her heart. She couldn't defend herself trapped inside.

But would outside in the wind be any better?

Madison turned and lifted her head up enough to peer over the seat back. The light came from the left side of the Jeep. If she exited on the right, could she position herself to take a shot if it reappeared? Maybe, but it was the only choice that gave her a chance.

Madison eased over to the rear passenger door and pulled the handle. It squeaked as cold air rushed inside the cab and she winced. As she flattened her back against the Jeep, she eased the door shut.

I can do this.

Madison crept toward the rear of the vehicle, pausing at the bumper. She brought the gun into a defensive shooting position, close to her body as her father taught her. She stepped clear of the vehicle.

A deep voice called out from the dark. "If you're gonna shoot me, just do it already."

"Identify yourself."

The man grunted and something fell into the snow. A light clicked on.

Madison sucked in a breath. He was clad in the black snowmobile gear of the men who chased her and Brianna, but from the grimace on his face and the pallor of his cheeks despite the freezing air, he wasn't in much of a position to attack.

He sat in the snow, one leg twisted awkwardly beneath him. The flashlight sat light up in the snow, creating an almost halo effect around his body. *Is he injured? Did he fall?* Madison couldn't risk letting her guard down. It could be a trap.

"Hands up." She stepped forward, gun aimed at his head.

He lolled over to the side, favoring his right leg as he shifted in the snow. "Like I said, either shoot me or not."

Madison aimed at his head. "Are you wearing a vest?"

"Just double tap, sweetheart." He tapped his own head to reinforce his words before reaching into his coat pocket.

Madison's finger twitched on the trigger.

He pulled out a small, soft-sided box and tapped it on his hand. He wasn't listening to her at all. Madison stepped forward as he shoved a cigarette into his mouth and lit it.

"Were you looking for us?"

"When?"

"Whenever."

He took a drag and blew the smoke toward the light. "Sure was."

"To kill us?"

"Maybe. Depended on what I found." He puffed again on the cigarette. "But it seems to me the tables have turned."

Madison couldn't get a read on the man at all. Was he serious? Did he actually expect her to shoot him in the head while he sat in the snow smoking? She looked past him toward the forest. "Anyone with you?"

"Not since you blew my cousin's brains out back there."

"Are you hurt?"

"Can't feel much of anything thanks to this snow."

He practically smirked at her as he sucked down another lungful of smoke.

They were getting nowhere. Madison advanced close enough to kick him if she wanted to. The snow tinged red around his right thigh and his pant leg gaped where a strip of duct tape was peeling. He was big, larger than she'd thought from her position by the Jeep.

He had to outweigh her by close to a hundred pounds. But he looked to be in bad shape. If the wound on his leg was serious, he could have lost a substantial amount of blood. Even the toughest NFL linebacker was no match for blood loss.

She had two choices: shoot him and ransack his body for anything useful or take a chance and see if they could help each other. The first option was the safe choice, and both she and the man knew it. But it wouldn't help her get out of the woods and it wouldn't keep her or Brianna warm enough overnight.

The plan hatching in her head was crazy; anyone would tell her that. But it just might work. She motioned at the Jeep. "I've got medical supplies."

"Rubbing it in before you shoot me?"

"Can you fix cars?"

He glanced past her to the Jeep lodged against the rocky outcrop. "Depends on how bad they're jacked up, but I'm not bad."

"How about a trade? I fix up your leg. You get that Jeep started."

"I hate to break it to you honey, but that Jeep isn't going anywhere."

"I don't need to drive it, I need to run the heater."

He took another drag before flicking the cigarette into the snow. It hissed and a trickle of smoke wafted into the air. "Can you help me up? This leg isn't good for much."

Madison lowered the gun and approached the man. "First wrong move you make and I'll shoot you. Don't doubt me."

"At this point, you'd be doing me a favor." He lurched to the side and held out his hand.

She took it and used all her strength to haul him up. Teetering on one leg, he almost collapsed. Madison rushed to slide her shoulder under his arm and take the weight off his injury. "Can you walk?"

"We'll find out." He took a step and groaned in pain, his weight almost bringing Madison to her knees. She erased his ability to take her out. If he couldn't walk without this much assistance, he couldn't kill her without a gun and so far, she hadn't seen one.

Together, they trudged through the snow to the Jeep. Madison stumbled, barely able to stay upright and keep the Glock in her hand. If she holstered it, she would be able to use both arms to hold him, but she couldn't give up the advantage.

Finally they reached the vehicle and he collapsed against the front left fender, sweat beading down his temple. "If you can pop the hood, I can take a look at the engine."

Madison struggled out from beneath his arm and opened the driver's door. Brianna shifted as the outside air hit her face, but she didn't wake up. Madison hit the button to disengage the hood catch and shut the door.

The man still leaned over the Jeep, gasping like a fish on a dock. Either he didn't see Brianna or he was in too much pain to care. Madison hurried around him, gun held low in her strong hand. Running her fingers back and forth beneath the dented hood, she found the release and lifted the hood.

"Grab the flashlight."

Madison hurried to fetch the flashlight still sitting out in the snow. By the time she stopped beside the Jeep and shined it on the engine, the man had sidled around the front and propped himself up on an oversized rock. "What happened when you tried to start it?"

"All it does is click."

The man nodded. "Do you have a tire iron?"

Madison leaned back and brought her gun closer to her body.

"Not to hit you with. I need to check the starter."

"You need a tire iron for that?"

He exhaled and looked at her like a disappointed teacher. "We could always go back to the double tap if that's easier."

Madison frowned, but did as he asked. She located the tire iron in the back of the Jeep and brought it up to him. After handing it over, she stepped well clear. "Now what?"

"Now I crawl under this damn thing and check it out."

Madison raised an eyebrow but didn't question it. If

he wanted to shimmy all two hundred pounds of him under the vehicle, he could have at it. At least she didn't have to worry about him shooting her from under there.

After a few agonizing minutes of watching him grunt and curse his way beneath the engine area, Madison jumped at a loud clang. "Did you just hit the engine?"

The noise sounded again before the man scooted out. He rolled over onto his back and tossed the tire iron into the snow. "Try it now."

While he lay in the snow, panting from pain, Madison stepped around him and up into the cab. She eased around Brianna and pressed her foot on the brake while she turned the key. The engine groaned and sputtered. She tried again. This time it held. He'd actually gotten it running.

She stepped down in shock. "What did you do?"

"I smacked the starter with the tire iron. The electrical contacts probably got stuck in the crash."

Madison didn't know where to begin. She reached down and held out her hand. "Thank you. My name's Madison Sloane."

He managed a smile despite the pain and closed his thick hand around hers. "Silas Cunningham."

With all her strength, she pulled Silas up to stand. "Let's get you into the back and take a look at that leg."

302 DAYS WITHOUT POWER

CHAPTER TWENTY

SILAS

Woods north of Truckee, CA

12:30 a.m.

"Damn it, woman. That hurt." Silas beat a fist against the door to the Jeep as the girl tightened the tourniquet around his leg.

"Shh." She chastised him for speaking too loudly and glanced up at the other girl in the front. Ever since Silas clambered into the back seat, the passed-out blonde hadn't done much more than roll over and moan. He opened his mouth to ask about her when pain shot through his thigh. He cursed.

"You need medical attention. The tourniquet can't be on too long or you'll lose your leg."

Silas snorted. "Don't worry. When I get back to town, I'll just pop into the nearest ER and, oh wait." He smacked his own face. "I might be dying, but I'm not delusional."

She leaned back. "The hospital might not be running, but that doesn't mean there aren't trained medical people around."

"Yeah? You got one hiding somewhere around here?"

The girl lapsed into silence.

"Madison, right?"

She nodded.

Silas leaned forward, grinding his teeth against the pain. "Well, *Madison*, how about you find me some whiskey and let me ride out the end with some dignity, huh?"

She shook her head and muttered something beneath her breath.

"What was that?"

Her eyes narrowed as she glanced up. "I guess your confidence is more bravado than courage, huh?"

It was Silas's turn to stay quiet.

"Thought so." She cleaned up the back of the Jeep without giving him another glance and climbed into the front.

Silas watched as she checked the other girl's pulse and pulled down the mylar blanket. Insulting him like that was stupid. If he had any strength left, he'd shoot her and her friend and be done with it. But as much as he hated to admit it, he needed her to patch him up first.

She didn't know what helping him meant, but she'd figure it out soon enough. He grunted as he leaned forward toward the driver's seat. "What's with your friend?"

Madison paused, eyebrows furrowed as she stared at the girl. "She got hurt in the crash."

"She gonna make it?"

"I hope so." Madison fumbled with something by her feet. "It's not whiskey, but it's all I've got." As she sat back up, she shoved a bottle of water in Silas's direction. "Thanks for getting the Jeep started."

He hesitated for a moment, uncomfortable with the act of kindness. After a moment, he snatched the bottle and barked out a reply. "You're welcome." From a purely selfish standpoint, he *was* thankful. Now he had a warm place to sit and figure out a plan. Sure as hell beat dying out in the snow from blood loss and exposure.

Madison tucked her hair behind her ear. "Are you one of the guys who attacked us on the road?"

He paused, water bottle halfway to his lips. "Thought you already knew the answer to that."

"Why us? We didn't do anything to you."

He snorted. "Tell that to Aaron back there in the snow."

"You were the ones who attacked. *You* set up the roadblock and chased us into the trees."

Silas shrugged and downed half the water bottle at once. "You had something we wanted."

"That's it? You just take whatever you want and screw everyone else?"

"It's been working so far."

She shook her head. "That's no way to live. What are you going to do when you run out of things to steal?"

Silas frowned. "What do you mean?"

"At some point, there's going to be nothing left to scavenge and no people left to steal from. How are you going to survive then?"

He shook his head. "That's easy. We'll hunt and fish and eat up all our stash."

"And when the forests are depleted and the streams are empty and your stash is all gone, then what?"

"I don't know, grow something."

Madison snorted. "Like it's that easy."

He motioned with the water bottle. "What, you know something about farming?"

"That's what I studied before the grid collapsed."

"In college?"

She nodded.

He leaned back and hooked his arms behind the seat. "I always wanted to go to college. My old man said it was a waste of time." He shook his head at the memory. "Turns out he was right."

"Don't say that. At some point we'll rebuild or foreign aid will show up. You can't lose hope that things will get better."

"You never went hungry before this shit show, did you?"

She scrunched up her nose. "What's that got to do with anything?"

"Working class stiffs like me and my family, we had it rough before the power went out. Not enough jobs, crappy pay." He almost smiled. "All the so-called stealing? We're just evening the score."

Her eyes widened. "Just because your life sucked doesn't give you the right to kill people and take what they have."

He picked a piece of dried blood off his hand. "Why not?"

"My parents worked hard to get where they were. I got scholarships to go to college. We might not have gone hungry, but we deserve the same chance to survive as you." She pursed her lips in disgust. "We've been through hell this past year."

Right. From the look of the fancy Jeep and the clean clothes she wore, Silas doubted she'd gone through anything half as bad as he'd seen. The fights over supplies and vehicles. The rioting in town. The strung-out drug addicts and alcoholics desperate for a fix. His own father.

He drained the rest of the water bottle and tossed it on the floorboard. "Tell me one crappy thing that's happened to you since the power failed."

"One of my best friends was killed in a gun fight."

Silas shrugged. "Wrong place, wrong time."

"Neighbors set my parents' house on fire and burned everything before attacking us. One of our friends died trying to escape."

He looked her up and down. "You seem all right."

She threw her hands out in disbelief. "People I know were murdered and we were forced out of our home because of arson and you act like it's nothing? What's happened to you that's so awful?"

"All of that and more. Twelve people in my family were killed before today. Probably up to twenty now, thanks to your group."

"They wouldn't have died if you hadn't blocked the road. You can't do bad things and expect people to be nice."

He shook his head. "All those people we've looted from? They wouldn't have made it anyway. We're just helping them get rid of their stuff a bit early, that's all."

"Who appointed you the decision-maker?"

"Guns and ammo, mostly."

Madison shook her head. "Weapons won't save you from bad timing. Part of my group was in a horrible car crash. Killed one instantly and led to the death of a bunch more."

"What's that got to do with guns?"

"The guy that hit them had a back seat full of them." She snorted. "Duffel bags crammed with guns are useless in a car crash. You'd be better off staying put and learning how to homestead instead of driving all over in a muscle car."

Silas stilled. "What kind of car?"

"I don't know." She blew him off. "Maybe a Camaro or a Mustang, what does it matter? The car isn't the point."

He shifted on the seat and lowered his right hand, struggling with the impossibility of the coincidence. What were the chances that this scrawny, spoiled, college girl's family ran into his father? A million to one?

It had to be someone else, some other man on a gun

run. Not his father. Not Butch Cunningham. No way would he survive the riots and the early days of chaos to die in a car accident on some back road. But if he did, and this girl or her family had something to do with it...

He wrapped his fingers around the gun tucked into the back of his pants. Silas would avenge his father's death. Even if it meant he would never make it out of the woods alive.

As calmly as he could, he looked her in the eye. "Where did you say this happened again?"

CHAPTER TWENTY-ONE

MADISON

Woods north of Truckee, CA

2:00 a.m.

Madison eased back in the seat. Fear pricked the hairs running down her neck and she swallowed hard. *What did I say?* She racked her brain, thinking through her brief recounting of the car crash. Guns and a muscle car.

Were they his? Did he know someone who left on a gun run and never came back?

She tried to remember what her father said about the guns they recovered. They were from some cult or group the Cliftons ran into when they first made it to the cabin. A nasty bunch of thugs who didn't care about grace or hospitality.

In time, they had been forgotten along with so many other things. Now, she desperately needed to remember.

Who are they? Madison squeezed her eyes shut,

willing the answer up from some recess in her mind. It wouldn't come. Whoever her father thought the guns belonged to, the name was gone. She opened her eyes.

Silas stared at her with unabashed hatred. His cheeks flushed and his neck muscles bunched as he sucked in a lungful of air. He teetered on the edge of control and a wave of panic rose up in Madison's chest.

I've got to get out of this.

She glanced around the Jeep. Thanks to Silas's injury, she could probably make it out the passenger door before he reached her, but that meant leaving Brianna behind. Madison couldn't do it.

Silas asked his question again. "Where was this crash?"

Madison licked her lips. "I don't know. I wasn't there."

"But you have some general idea, right? Was it in California? Montana? New York?"

"Somewhere around here, I think." Madison eyeballed the console. The handgun sat in the tray, no more than six inches from her right hand and Silas's knee. She had set it down to treat Silas's wound. *So stupid.* The rifle lay on the passenger floorboard behind her. She couldn't grab either one without it being obvious. She cursed herself.

"What color was the car?"

Madison looked up at the man. Frustration and pain turned his voice sharp. A shimmer of sweat broke out across his forehead and glinted in the flashlight glow. He had to be in terrible pain, but for some reason the car crash mattered more.

I have to stall and find a way out. She eased to her right. "I don't know anything about the car."

"You said it was a muscle car. What kind?"

"I don't know. You'd have to ask someone who was there."

"They live with you?"

Shit, shit, shit. Why did I say that? She stammered. "N-No. I mean, they used to, but—" She scrambled for some way to deflect the questioning. "You just attacked us. For all I know, my family and friends are dead. We could be all that's left."

Silas wiped a hand down his face, lingering on his tangled beard. "Then tell me everything they told you about the crash. Don't leave anything out."

She swallowed and shifted again in the seat, hoping to angle her body enough to hide the visual on the rifle with her hips. There was no way to go for the Glock without risking a physical fight, and Silas outweighed her by close to a hundred pounds. The rifle was her only option. *I have to distract him.*

Madison cleared her throat. "They were driving down a rural road in two vehicles. An old pickup truck was in front. The vehicle following the pickup spotted a car on a side road."

She hacked up a dry cough and leaned over.

"Don't stop."

"I'm thirsty."

"You'll be a hell of a lot worse if you don't finish."

She coughed harder. "Just give me—" Madison stretched her arm behind her, fingers brushing cold metal.

"Pick up that rifle and I'll put a bullet through your temple and watch it turn your brain to mush."

Madison froze, hand hovering a few inches above the stock. As she twisted back to look at Silas, he pulled out a handgun. Her hope crumbled. *I should have gone for the Glock. At least then I'd have a chance.*

Silas rested the full-size piece on his knee, hand perched on top, finger easy on the trigger. "Tell me what happened."

She curled her fingers into a fist to quell a tremor and sat back up. "I saved your life. If it weren't for me, you'd be frozen out there in the snow."

"That's the only reason you aren't dead yet." He grimaced as he shifted his wounded leg's position. "Now spill it."

She exhaled and told him everything she knew. "At some point the roads intersected. The car running along the side road entered the intersection at the same time as the pickup. It T-boned it at a high rate of speed. The pickup flipped a bunch of times." She swallowed, remembering how Dani wrapped her arms around her middle when she told the story. "Two of the passengers died on impact, a third died a few hours later. The driver was thrown through the windshield and lived."

"What about the car?"

Madison sniffed. "It was wrecked. Had to be going a hundred when it hit the truck. No way anyone could survive." She left out the part about Dani finding the driver wheezing out his last few breaths. Madison tried to soften the blow. "It was a car accident. No one could have seen it coming."

Silas pressed the fingers of his free hand to his temple. "So it was a muscle car, traveling on some small road, somewhere near here. That's it? That's all you've got?"

"I wasn't there. This happened months ago. Way back in the early days."

He shot forward. "When exactly?"

Madison looked up to the roof of the Jeep, trying to remember when her father came back with Colt, Dani, and Larkin in tow. "We were still clearing the field for the farm, so it had to be spring. Maybe a month after the power went out? It couldn't have been much more."

Silas shook his head. "You're lying. There's something you're not telling me. Something you remember." He reached forward, trying to grab at her shirt or hands.

Madison shied back. "That's it, I swear."

Silas rose up from the back seat and Madison reached for the Glock. Her fingers wrapped around the cold metal as Silas charged through the two seats. He slammed the butt of his gun on her fingers and bones snapped.

Madison screamed and yanked her hand back as he lifted the Glock from the console.

Brianna moaned and rolled toward her in the driver's

seat. Words lolled out of her mouth, thick and syrupy. "What's... the... big... idea?"

Pain radiated out from the center of Madison's index and middle fingers. She inhaled through her nose and out through her mouth as her vision ringed in black. "Brianna, wake up!" She needed her friend's help or they were both going to die.

"I don't wanna." Brianna's blonde curls fell across her face as she rolled over. "Wake me when the movie's over."

Madison cursed. "It's not a movie. I need you to wake up."

Brianna didn't move. The blow to her head and the injury to her leg had rendered her useless. Madison knew that modern medicine recommended letting concussion patients sleep, so that's what she'd done. But now she wished she'd tried to wake her up.

"Your friend can't help you." Silas pointed his gun straight at Madison's face. "Tell me everything or I'll shoot you both, right now."

Fear closed Madison's throat. She couldn't breathe, couldn't think. She'd helped this man and now he was going to kill her for a car accident she didn't see with people she didn't meet until after it happened. It was crazy. His finger tightened around the trigger and Madison blurted out the first thing in her mind. "If I had been there, I could tell you more, but that's all Colt said about it!"

"Who's Colt?"

Shit. Pain radiated out from her hand and she couldn't think. If she'd had more control of her faculties, she would have used a fake name or come up with some lie to throw him off, but the pain rendered her incapable. A faint ringing sounded in her left ear and her vision dimmed even more. She was on the verge of passing out.

Madison forced out the words. "One of the members of my group."

"Is he still alive?"

"I don't know. He was in the U-Haul."

Silas leaned back and Madison shivered. Whatever was going through his head couldn't be good. She needed a way out and fast. Madison gritted her teeth and fought off the impending blackout. She had to stay conscious.

The rifle still sat on the floor behind her. If she could reach it... She lifted her hand and groaned. The only hand that could reach the rifle had two smashed fingers. It was hopeless.

She struggled against the pain as the ringing in her ears intensified. Her vision narrowed to a circle, fuzzed out to black around the edges. She swooned and fell back against the dashboard. It was all she could do to blink and breathe.

That's when she saw it. *A light.*

Small and round, it could only be a flashlight beam. She struggled to focus on the little circle of light. Sooner or later, the person attached to it would see the Jeep. They had to hear the engine by now. A surge of energy pushed back against the pain and dizziness threatening to pull her under.

Please be my dad, please. Madison almost smiled in relief at the thought and let her eyes slip closed. The darkness enveloped her and the ringing in her ears rose to a crescendo. The throbbing in her hand settled into a *one-two-three, one-two-three* rhythm like a bad waltz she hadn't tried since dance class in the fifth grade.

"This could be our way out." She didn't realize she said the words out loud. She rolled to the side, reaching for Brianna. "This is it. We'll be saved." They could finally go home where it was warm and safe and someone loved them. She slumped over when a blast of cold air jolted her out of the haze of pain.

Madison blinked. Reality came back into focus: the front seat, Brianna's unconscious form, the angry man in the back seat. Fear launched a fresh wave of adrenaline through her bloodstream as she looked up at the open door, but it was too late.

The butt of a gun slammed into her temple and she fell against the steering wheel. Not even the sound of the Jeep's horn could keep her from passing out.

CHAPTER TWENTY-TWO

WALTER

Woods north of Truckee, CA

2:00 a.m.

Damn it. Snow slipped under the waistband of Walter's ski pants and into the top of his boots. He shivered as the ice crystals melted on his bare skin. Thanks to faulty batteries, his flashlight ran out of juice hours ago. Ever since then, he'd been walking blind.

He'd tried to stay in the tire tracks from the Jeep, but every once in a while, he'd list to the left or right. After the second run-in with a tree trunk, he'd taken to holding his hands out in front of him and waving them about every four paces.

The chances of finding Brianna and Madison without even the moon for light were slim, but he couldn't stop. Hunkering down meant death. Walter had to keep his blood flowing and heart pumping through the freezing night. If he didn't come across the Jeep before dawn, he planned to backtrack to the road and hope Colt left another snowmobile intact and drivable.

Walter pulled himself out of a two-foot-deep snow drift and stomped on the ground. Melted snow trickled down his ankle and welled in the front of his boot. His toes didn't react. He tried to wiggle them. *Nothing.*

Fear of frostbite couldn't stop him now. He shoved the images of chopping off dead toes out of his mind and scrambled back onto the hard-packed snow of the Jeep's tracks. Madison needed him more than Walter needed a few toes. They weren't good for much, anyway.

On he trudged, more careful and slower than before. The tracks seemed to curve as trees crowded against the dark night sky, deepening the blackness in front of him. A single sound cut the stillness.

A car horn.

Walter spun in a circle. Was it the Jeep? One of the men who ambushed them? Colt and Larkin in trouble? Thanks to the topography and the denseness of the forest, he couldn't pinpoint the direction of the noise. Left? Right? North? South?

It could have come from anywhere. He stood still, straining to listen for any further clues. He was concentrating so hard on his ears, he almost missed the sight in front of him.

A tiny prick of light danced across his vision. At first he thought he imagined it, so he shut his eyes and counted to ten. When he opened them again, it was back, bobbing and weaving and growing larger by the second.

A flashlight. Walter hurried toward the trees. He didn't know if the light came from the direction of the horn or how many people were headed his way. Without a light of his own, he was at a massive disadvantage. He unslung the rifle from his shoulder and yanked off a glove. The cold air bit at his chapped skin as he slipped his finger around the trigger.

Shooting blind would get him nowhere. What if it was Madison, hurt and trudging through the snow? He had to get a visual on the person holding the flashlight, but he had to do it from the protection of the trees. His free hand made contact with a sturdy trunk and Walter ducked behind it.

Minutes ticked by and the light grew larger, eventually flattening out into an oval on the snow. It kept to the same tracks Walter had tried to follow, every so often panning into the trees and back down. His shoe prints were mostly invisible in the portions where the Jeep's tires hard-packed the snow, but on the edges where he stumbled, they had to be obvious.

The flashlight beam rose, sweeping across the trees where Walter hid. He held his breath. The beam of light passed him by.

After a few more minutes, it came to rest on a bulky shape in the snow. A rock or something buried. Walter squinted, trying to see what the other person found. The flashlight beam grew smaller and more focused, stopping on something black and mechanical. It took Walter a moment to place it: a caterpillar tread stuck up in the snow.

The shape wasn't a rock; it was a snowmobile.

Walter would never have seen it in the dark. He stayed still, watching as the person wielding the flashlight dug the vehicle out of the snow. After a few minutes, the flashlight beam wavered and shifted, changing from a concentrated beam to a dim lantern.

Thanks to the flashlight's position handle-down in the snow, the light reflected in a wide circle and Walter could finally see the person hunched over the rig. It wasn't Madison. The man was large, easily outweighing Walter by fifty pounds or more, and he moved like he was accustomed to hard labor.

His oversized shoulders bunched as he rocked the snowmobile back and forth. *One, two, three, four.* The arc of the snowmobile increased with each grunting effort.

At last, it flipped over onto the skis and tread. Walter exhaled. *This could be my chance.* Walter crept forward, careful to keep to the cover of the thicker trees, as the man brushed the snow and ice off the controls.

Walter paused. The snowmobile was Walter's best hope of finding Madison. He needed that rig, but he needed it running. He slowed, waiting as the man turned the key and reached for the choke.

The man yanked the cord a handful of times and cursed. Ten feet of snow and trees separated them. Walter held his breath. *Any second now.* The man reached for the cord pull again and yanked.

The snowmobile engine sputtered and groaned to life and Walter took a step out of the tree line, toward the rig.

He hadn't moved more than a foot when the barrel of a gun jabbed into his temple.

"Take another step and I blow your brains all over the snow."

Walter ground his teeth together. He'd been so focused on the snowmobile, wanting so badly for it to start, that he'd lost perspective. Rule number one of any encounter was to maintain situational awareness, and he'd failed. The cold had turned him sloppy and desperate.

He side-eyed the man holding a gun to his head. From the corner of his eye, all Walter could make out was a bulky shape much like the man now standing beside the snowmobile holding a handgun of his own. He pointed it at Walter.

Even if Walter had been able to take out the man holding the gun to his head, he'd never be able to take out the one by the snowmobile, too. He was caught and didn't see a way out.

The gun pressed against Walter's temple inched in harder as the man holding it called out. "That thing gonna work?"

"Hell if I know, but it's runnin' now, ain't it?" The man standing by the snowmobile reached down and lifted the flashlight out of the snow. He pointed it straight at Walter's face. "Where'd he come from?"

"Found him lurking in the trees watching you work. You should be more careful, Donny. If I hadn't spotted him, he'd have taken you out."

"Like hell he would have." Donny spat on the ground. "I can handle myself all right."

"Get the snowmobile over to the Jeep."

"What are we gonna do with him?"

"Depends on who he is and what he's got."

The gun eased back enough for Walter to turn his head. Thanks to the flashlight beam in his face, he couldn't see a thing. His rifle was snatched from his grip and a pair of meaty hands patted him all over before removing his handgun stashed in an appendix holster.

"He's clean."

The flashlight beam lowered and Walter tried to blink away the spots.

"Start walking, buddy."

"I can't see."

"You don't need to see. You need to walk." A gun barrel poked him again in the shoulder. Probably his own rifle. "Move."

Walter took one step and then another. Every so often, the rifle's barrel would poke one of his shoulders and he would correct his path. The snowmobile revved behind him and darted out into the clearing. The single headlight lit up the tracks in front and Walter's chest seized.

The Jeep.

It couldn't have been more than two hundred yards ahead. Even from that distance, he could see the damage. Mangled hood. Broken axle. For all he knew, neither Brianna nor Madison survived the crash.

He forced his feet to keep moving even though his

heart willed him to stop. He didn't want to know if his daughter was dead. He didn't want to face that future. It was all his fault. He was the one who told her to go. He was the one who put her in harm's way. If she and Brianna had stayed with the U-Haul, they would all be home now, safe and sound.

But he told them to run. He'd been scared and foolish and now his daughter might be dead.

The snowmobile pulled up alongside its twin and Donny swung his leg over the seat. He turned and waited for Walter and the man holding him at gunpoint to catch up.

The man behind him jabbed the gun into the small of Walter's back as they entered the headlight beam of the snowmobile. "That's far enough."

Walter stopped. The man eased around him and Walter got a look at him for the first time. As big as Donny, but older. Bushy beard, skull cap pulled down tight over his head. Blood coated one leg and as he took another step Walter noticed an obvious limp.

The man was injured. He turned to Walter. "You from the U-Haul?"

"Don't know what you're talking about." Walter clasped his naked hand with the one still wearing a glove. His fingers burned from the cold.

"You ever seen this Jeep before?"

Walter shook his head. "Nope."

The man looked him up and down. "I don't believe you."

"Believe what you want. I was just out here, looking

for something to scavenge. Saw the snowmobile and thought I'd take it."

"You got a cabin near here?"

Walter shook his head. "I'm a nomad."

"No one scavenges in the middle of the night in the woods when it's this cold."

"I do."

"Bullshit." The man turned to his buddy. "Donny, drag 'em out. If he won't admit to who he is the easy way, maybe we can change his mind."

CHAPTER TWENTY-THREE
WALTER

Woods north of Truckee, CA
2:00 a.m.

Donny yanked open the driver's-side door to the Jeep. A shock of blonde curls fell out of the seat, followed by the slumped-over body of Brianna. She landed in a whoosh of snow.

Walter swallowed. He couldn't tell from that distance if Brianna was unconscious and alive or already dead. A purpling bruise spread out across her forehead and a goose egg the size of a tennis ball swelled above her temple.

"Recognize her?"

He leaned in. "Can't say for sure." His voice warbled and Walter bit the inside of his cheek. He had to keep them guessing. "I see a lot of strays in the woods."

"Bring out the other one."

Donny reached out and grabbed Brianna by the wrists. He dragged her over to the idle snowmobile and dumped her in the snow. Walter strained to listen. Was that a groan? He couldn't hear over the rumble of the engine.

He watched as Donny huffed back over to the Jeep and reached inside. Madison's brown hair spilled over his arm as he dragged her headfirst out of the vehicle.

Walter hissed. His daughter was injured. Blood clotted in her hair and stuck to her cheek. He wanted more than anything to rush to her and check for a pulse, but that meant death for both of them.

Donny tilted her body toward him and let him stare at Madison's face. She wasn't pale or slightly blue and her body showed no signs of rigor. But that didn't mean she was still breathing.

Walter turned to the man with the gun. He hoped the sweat beading across his forehead didn't give him away. "Don't know her either." He chose his next words carefully. "You found them like this?"

"If you don't know them, what do you care?"

"Just curious."

Donny dragged Madison over to the snowmobile and dumped her next to Brianna. "Ain't you ever heard of curiosity killed the cat?"

"I'm not a cat."

"And I'm not an idiot." The man with the gun stepped forward. "Who are you and who are these girls?"

Walter took a step back and held up his hands. It took

all his self-control not to charge, gun be damned. "I was just looking for something to steal. That's all."

"Just shoot him and be done with it, Silas." Donny could have been a five-year-old whining for ice cream. "My balls are about to fall off."

"Get that brown-haired one." Silas motioned to Madison. "Haul her over here."

Walter clenched his fists. "I told you, I don't know them."

"Then you won't care what I do to them." Silas waited while Donny hoisted Madison up and half-dragged her over.

"Prop her up. I want him to get a real good look."

Donny gripped Madison around the waist and hauled her into a standing position. She sagged against his shoulder and her head lolled back. The sight of his daughter so fragile and unprotected kicked his heart into overdrive.

Silas reached out with his free hand and stroked Madison's cheek. "She's a real beauty, this one. Helpful, too. She fixed up my leg when I was about to bleed out all over the back seat. But it turns out her friends did a real bad thing."

Walter sucked in a breath through clenched teeth, air sawing in and out as he teetered on the brink of losing control. "What's that?"

Silas reached out and grabbed a handful of Madison's hair. "Maybe you know the story." He twisted her hair in his fist and yanked.

Madison moaned.

Walter gave a start. *Oh my God. She's alive. Madison is alive.* He fought down the rising emotion. Knowing she was alive changed everything. He had to concentrate and focus on Silas's words. He had to find a way to save her.

Silas kept talking, twisting Madison's hair until it pulled at her scalp. "Silver Camaro full of weapons and ammo." He lifted up Walter's rifle. "Guns just like this. My father left last spring on a gun run and he never came home."

Walter reeled.

Could it be? He thought back to the day that he stumbled across Colt in the forest. He'd found them after the car crash, but it didn't take long for more men to show up looking. And they weren't just any men, but members of Cunningham's group. If the man in the Camaro was this bastard's father, then Silas was a Cunningham, too.

Madison was in much deeper danger than he'd thought.

He tried to play it off. "Seems pretty crazy, if you ask me. The chances of running into your father's killer out here in the woods."

Silas must have caught the shock on Walter's face. He leaned forward, his lips brushing Madison's cheek.

Anger surged through Walter's veins and he leaned in. "Stop it." The words rushed out before Walter could hold them back.

Silas turned to him, a smile on his lips. "Why? I thought she was a stray."

"She is." Walter could barely speak. "Doesn't mean I like you disrespecting women. She looks like a kid."

"Well, which is she? A woman or a child?" Silas leaned in and took a sniff of Madison's hair. "Smells like a woman to me." He leaned down and unzipped her jacket. It fell open to reveal a tight-fitting sweater. He ran his hand down her front, pausing on her chest. "Feels like a woman."

Walter took a step forward. He would die before that man laid another hand on her. "I told you to stop."

Silas ran his tongue along the front of his teeth, pushing his lower lip out as he stared at Walter. "So is she your girlfriend or your daughter?"

Walter snapped. The roar that rushed up his throat and burst from his lips sounded more animal than human. He rushed at the man holding Madison, but it was no use. Silas used his massive weight advantage to bust Walter across the head. The butt of the rifle landed hard on Walter's temple and he slammed into the snow.

His entire face was buried in the icy powder and he spit out a mouthful as he tried to breathe. Silas stepped over and kicked him in the side. Walter rolled over onto his back, clutching his head where the gun made impact.

The whole world spun. Nausea threatened to turn his stomach inside out. He could barely see. His ears rung. He tried to lift his head, but the shooting pain forced him back to the ground. He couldn't move, let alone stand.

Donny whined again. "Just shoot him, man. This chick's heavy."

"Complain again and we'll have matching bullet wounds."

Walter rolled over to see Silas motion to the running snowmobile. "There's a tarp in my saddlebag. Use it to wrap them up, then tie them to the back. They should fit on that rear rack just fine."

"What about him?"

Silas smiled and turned to Walter. "Don't worry. I've got something in mind."

With a gun digging into his throbbing temple, Walter managed only limited resistance as Donny tied his hands behind his back and propped him up against the closest tree.

He sat in the snow, slowly regaining his faculties while Silas raided the Jeep and Donny wrapped Madison and Brianna in a tarp.

Every minute that ticked by sharpened Walter's senses and steeled his resolve. He wasn't letting them leave. He would die before his daughter ended up at the mercy of the Cunningham clan.

When Donny finished securing the girls to the snowmobile, they looked like a giant burrito that barely fit on the rack. One wrong move and Madison or Brianna would hit the ground or a tree and be dead on impact.

Donny stomped over, chubby fingers wrapped around Walter's own handgun. "Can I shoot him now?"

Silas climbed up onto the seat of the snowmobile and turned to Donny. "Get that other snowmobile started and head out as soon as you can."

Donny turned in alarm. "What? You're leaving without me?"

"Not my fault it took you so long to load this precious

cargo." Silas looked back at the lumpy tarp. "Get your sled running. Wait for it to warm up and then follow me."

"What about him?"

Silas grinned. "Leave him. He can freeze to death imagining all the fun we're gonna have tonight."

Donny's eyes widened. "Sweet." He almost licked his lips. "I'll be right behind you." He hustled to the snowmobile and turned the key as Silas squeezed the gas. The snowmobile shot forward and Walter's stomach heaved.

I have to find a way. His head throbbed as he looked at Donny. Way heavier than Walter and armed with at least a handgun, the man posed a serious challenge. But with Silas driving off into the dark, Walter was out of options.

He tugged on the rope holding his hands. It loosened but didn't come free. While Donny climbed on the snowmobile, Walter rose up onto his knees and pushed his arms down as far as possible. Wiggling back and forth, he managed to slide his tied hands beneath his butt. Falling onto his back, he pulled first one leg and then the other through the loop of his arms.

Sweat coated his face, but he could move and he didn't have much time. The snowmobile was running. Walter clambered to his feet. It was only him and Donny now and Walter knew who was going to win.

He charged at the big man leaning over the sled and hit him full force in the back. With an *oof,* Donny slammed into the handlebars. Walter kneed him in the back, one, two, three times, rocking with all his weight before striking again.

Donny twisted around, fumbling with the gun, but Walter wasted no time. He scrambled up onto the seat of the snowmobile and scrabbled for Donny's head. His arms looped over the man's face and the rope still tied tight around his wrists jammed against Donny's neck.

Walter yanked hard enough to pull them both off the sled and into the snow. He tightened his grip on Donny's neck, sawing the rope into the big man's flesh. Donny rolled over him, kicking and flailing as Walter crushed his airway.

Fingers clawed at Walter's hand, digging in and ripping his frozen skin. Walter pulled the rope tighter. "You think you're going to touch my daughter? That your hands would get within an inch of her skin?"

Donny gurgled and Walter rolled him forward. The gun fell into the snow and Walter released his death grip. He slipped the rope off Donny's neck and the big man gagged and coughed, his face purple from lack of oxygen. Walter dug the gun out of the snow and crawled over to Donny. He jammed the barrel so tight against his forehead, the skin around it turned white.

"Where did Silas go?"

Donny sputtered.

"If you don't tell me by the time I count to three, I'll shoot you in the foot. One, two, three."

Walter whipped the gun down and stabbed the meaty part of Donny's boot and fired. The guy screamed.

"I've got fifteen rounds. When I'm done with your feet and hands, I'll work my way up."

Tears streamed out of Donny's eyes and he tried to speak. "He... took... them..." He erupted in a gurgling cough.

Walter twisted around and shoved the gun against Donny's other foot. "One."

"Donner... Lake. We live at the lake."

"Where exactly?"

"An old motel. Donner Lake Motor Court."

"What's your name?"

"D-Donny."

"Your whole name."

"Donald Henry Cunningham."

Walter clamped his jaw shut. It was true. Madison and Brianna were on their way to Cunningham's camp. The men who ambushed them on the road were part of Cunningham's crew. It could always be worse, but in the moment, Walter wasn't sure how.

He lifted his gun off Donny's boot, took aim, and buried two bullets in his skull.

CHAPTER TWENTY-FOUR

TRACY

Northwoods Boulevard

3:00 a.m.

"Did you hear that?"

"Sounded like gunshots."

"A pair." Tracy pointed toward the forest. "From that direction."

Peyton crouched low behind a snowmobile turned on its side. "You think we should check it out?"

Tracy clicked off her flashlight and plunged the road into darkness. Without a moon that night, the forest darkened the road to the point of blindness and she blinked, barely able to tell when her eyes were open or closed. She slid over to Peyton, boots kicking up gravel and bits of asphalt as she hid.

A low hum sounded in her right ear and Tracy shook her head. "Is that an engine?"

Peyton's parka rustled beside her. "Maybe. Too quiet to tell."

Tracy didn't like it. They had managed to find the scene of the shootout without too much trouble, but since then, their search had been hopeless. Hours of driving up and down the roadway in Ben's shot-up F-150 followed by more hours on foot.

Without Colt or Larkin to guide them, it was impossible. Tracks led off in almost every direction from the road. Tracy had followed one set for hours, convinced it would lead them straight to Walter and Madison. It turned out to be a wild goose chase, leading them at last right back to where they started on the road. All they knew was that Walter was on a snowmobile and the girls were in the Jeep. It simply wasn't enough to go on.

Tracy exhaled and listened to the mechanical hum. "I think it's coming our way." She shifted her weight on her feet and reached for a shotgun hanging from a strap across her body. "We should be ready. If that's one of the men from the ambush coming back, we need to catch him and find out where they're from."

She steadied herself, gripping the shotgun tight in her thin gloves, waiting. The hum turned into a groan and grunt of an engine. Moments later, a single headlight pierced the tree line. Tracy held her breath.

The snowmobile headed for the road, headlight wobbling this way and that.

"I don't think that's one of the men." Peyton's voice was full of doubt. "He doesn't look like a good driver."

Tracy pressed her lips together. She refused to let the

hope pawing at her insides in. She couldn't risk the disappointment if the driver heading their way wasn't Walter.

At last, the vehicle broke through the trees, headlight blinding, as it turned. It shimmied in the roughed-up snow beside the road, bouncing over tracks from the skirmish. As the driver tried to accelerate toward the north and the rising terrain, the snowmobile bucked.

One ski came off the ground. The driver leaned the wrong way and as Tracy and Peyton watched, the whole sled flipped over and landed in the snow. The tread on the back kept spinning, flinging bits of ice into the air.

"Come on," Tracy whispered to Peyton as she eased into the road. "Let's get a better look."

Peyton followed a few steps behind as Tracy made her way closer and closer to the upended vehicle. As she cleared the back end, a man emerged from the snow. He shut off the snowmobile and cursed himself.

Tracy recognized the voice. "Walter? Is that you?"

The man spun around and lifted a pair of glasses off his eyes. "Tracy?"

She ran for him, high stepping through the snow, until she collided with his sturdy frame. "Thank God you're all right." She wrapped her arms around him and squeezed.

"I won't be much longer if you crush my lungs."

Tracy let Walter go and laughed. "Sorry." She peered in the direction that he came. "Tell me you found our daughter. Tell me the girls are all right."

Walter held out a hand. Even in the stratified light from the snowmobile, Tracy could see him shaking.

Tracy's insides seized. "What is it? What's happened?"

Peyton stomped up beside Tracy. "Are they dead?"

Walter shook his head. "No. They're alive and I know where they've been taken."

Tracy clutched at her middle. "Taken? By whom?"

"The Cunninghams. That's who ambushed us in the road."

"What?" Tracy palmed her forehead and looked out at the forest. The Cliftons had run into a few of Cunningham's men while scavenging in the early days before Tracy and her family arrived. They had talked about how dangerous and brutal they were and convinced everyone to stay far, far away.

Colt, Larkin, and Dani were the only ones to even encounter some of the clan, and it had been months ago. She couldn't believe the news. If what the Cliftons had said about Cunningham was true, Madison and Brianna were in grave danger.

She turned back to her husband. "Was it Cunningham who ambushed you on the road?"

"I'm afraid so. We took out a good number of his men, but the rest are all living in an old motel on the shores of Donner Lake. I know where it is. It's where they've taken the girls."

"What are they going to do to them?" Peyton voiced the question Tracy didn't dare consider.

"Nothing good."

"Then we need to go. We can hit them before they even know we're coming."

"It's not that simple. You remember all the guns Dani recovered from that car. If we show up, just the three of us, we'll not only get ourselves killed, but we'll be signing Madison and Brianna's death warrants."

Peyton agreed. "No one else knows where they are. If something happens to us, they'll be on their own."

"Then go home and tell everyone, but I'm not waiting. I have to save my daughter." Tracy took a step toward the truck, but Walter reached out and grabbed her arm.

"We only have one chance to save them, Tracy." He closed the distance between them. "We have to do this the smart way."

Tracy sobbed. Her whole body urged her to go, to chase down whoever took her only child and make them pay. But her husband was right. She would only get them both killed. "We have to be fast, Walter. Every minute she's out there..."

"I know." He clutched her tight, his lips brushing against her ear. Walter dropped his voice so only Tracy could hear. "I will do whatever it takes to get them back. You have my word."

She pulled away. "Let's go. We need to plan."

Together, Tracy, Peyton, and Walter piled into the F-150 and Tracy punched the gas. It would take at least half an hour if not more to make it back to the Cliftons' farm and a few hours to prepare.

She checked her watch. They wouldn't be ready until close to sunrise. She prayed they wouldn't be too late.

Right on her internal schedule, Tracy whipped the F-150 into the Cliftons' farm just as the her watch turned to 4:00. She shoved the truck into park and blasted the horn three times.

Colt and Dani were the first to emerge, followed by Larkin and Brianna's parents. They all stood on the porches to the cabins, waiting.

Tracy hurried to meet them. "Madison and Brianna have been kidnapped."

Anne covered her mouth with her hand. Barry's cheeks flushed in anger. "Who took them?"

Walter stopped beside Tracy. "The Cunninghams. That's who ambushed us with the roadblock."

Barry's face slipped from red to white in a matter of seconds. "Then it's too late. They'll be dead already."

"Don't say that." Tracy turned to Barry. "We're going to rescue them."

"How?" Anne looked up at her husband, echoing his fear. "There's fifty of them at least, all built like tanks and stockpiled with weapons. We even step foot near the lake and we're asking to get strung up by our feet and left for the bears. We almost died when we ran into a group of them in Truckee."

Tracy slammed a fist into her palm. "We are going to get them back."

"We need all the guns and ammo we can carry and more besides." Larkin motioned to Peyton. "Help me get everything together." The two set off for the weapons shed and Tracy exhaled in relief.

Colt nodded. "We'll need diversions, too. Dani and I can get started making up some smoke bombs. We can do what we did in Eugene and flush them out." They took off, leaving Tracy and Walter and the Cliftons alone.

Walter reached for Tracy's hand and gave it a squeeze before turning to Anne and Barry. "I know this is scary, but Colt, Larkin, and I are no stranger to combat. We can do this. We can get our daughters back."

Barry nodded, but his expression was still grim. "We'll go together. All of us."

"What about Ben?"

"We can set him up with supplies." Barry glanced at his wife. "We need to be prepared for the worst-case scenario, not just for Ben, but for all of us."

Tracy volunteered. "That Brianna and Madison are already dead?"

"No. That we're signing our death warrants. If we don't kill every last Cunningham in that place, we'll never be able to sleep again. They will hunt us down. They will make us pay. It's what they do."

Walter nodded. "The one I spoke to said as much. It's why he took Madison and Brianna. He blames them for his father's death."

Tracy stayed silent as Walter explained what he'd learned to Barry and Anne. When he finished, Barry nodded in understanding. "It's their code. Even before the grid collapsed they were like that. The old man lived not that far from here in a shack up north of the ski resorts. If he thought you wronged him, he never forgot it."

Anne nodded. "A few years ago one of his dogs was hit by a car. He was convinced Spencer, a nice old man who lived on the resort property, was responsible." She pulled her coat tighter as she recalled the memory. "Spencer woke up one morning to find all his chickens slaughtered and his horses missing. He died not long after."

Tracy exhaled. "And it's the same Cunningham who's in charge now?"

"His son, from what I can tell."

"Then we can't waste anymore time. We need to hit them and hit them hard. Our daughters aren't going to end up like those chickens."

Barry's voice cracked as he spoke. "If we don't get there in time, they'll end up a hell of a lot worse."

CHAPTER TWENTY-FIVE

MADISON

Somewhere near Truckee, CA

5:00 a.m.

"What the..."

A groan sounded from somewhere nearby and Madison rolled onto her side. A sharp pain lanced her hand and she clutched it tight to her chest.

"Where the hell are we?" Brianna's voice cut through the throbbing and Madison managed to sit up.

"Wherever Silas decided to take us, I guess."

"Who is Silas?"

Madison blinked. She couldn't see much in the dark. Using her good hand as a guide she stood and felt around. Wood table. Four chairs. Old tube TV on a bench. Bed with a bouncy, squeaky mattress. Ashtray full of cigarette butts.

She recoiled with a grimace and opened the drawer

to the bedside table. "Yes!" She clicked on the small flashlight and a weak beam of light illuminated the space. The room was just as she'd felt in the dark: old and run-down. "I think we're in a motel."

Brianna groaned. "A really nasty motel." She picked her fingers up from the floor. "The carpet is gritty."

Madison shined the light on the floor. What had once been brown indoor-outdoor carpet now looked like worn down strips of Velcro stapled to the floor. "Maybe this room was scheduled for renovation before the EMP."

"Or maybe this Silas guy is a slob." Brianna looked around the room. "Where are our jackets?"

Madison glanced down at her sweater and jeans. "I don't want to know. We need to get out of here." She walked over to the windows and clicked off the light. It was still dark, but judging by the pale coloring of the sky on the edge of the forest, dawn wasn't that far off. "We can't be here when they come looking for us."

"Why not?"

Madison turned to Brianna. "Because whatever they have in mind, it'll be bad." She filled her best friend in on what happened after she passed out. When she got to the part about Silas turning on her, Brianna cursed.

"So you saving his life didn't matter?"

"Apparently not." Madison eased down onto the edge of the bed. The flashlight lit up a stain streaked across the lower half of the comforter and she stood back up. "He thinks we're to blame. He's going to be taking out his anger on us."

Brianna tugged a hair elastic off her wrist and

wrapped up her hair into a tight bun. "Then let's go. You scope out the windows. I'll try the front door."

She leaned forward on her knee and tried to stand. She didn't make it more than halfway up before collapsing in pain. "Damn it." She slammed her palm on the ground. "I forgot about my leg."

Madison walked over and crouched beside Brianna's left leg. The swelling in her knee was almost gone. "In the Jeep your knee was huge. Are you sure it's your leg that's broken and not something in your knee?"

"I don't know."

"What about your head? You were out of it in the Jeep. I tried to wake you up, but I couldn't."

"I have a nasty headache, but other than that, I'm alive." Brianna pointed at Madison's head. "You don't look so good yourself. Try to help me up."

Madison held out her good arm and Brianna tried to stand. She shook her head and eased back to the floor. "It hurts like a you-know-what as soon as I put weight on it."

"Then we'll have to rig up a splint." Madison spun around, searching for something she could use. The flashlight beam lit up old, painted cabinets with one knob missing. A kitchenette with a wood-paneled mini-fridge and a single burner on the Formica counter. A small closet with sliding doors.

"Here!" She rushed to the closet and popped the wooden closet rod out of the slots on the wall. "We can secure your leg to this to stabilize it."

"I don't think that will work."

"We won't know unless we try."

Madison brought the rod over and set it beside Brianna's leg. "Try and straighten it out."

Brianna clenched a fist as she lowered her leg toward the floor. A few inches away, she shook her head. "I can't do it. It hurts too much. I need some sort of crutch." She grabbed the closet rod. "How about this? Can we make it into a crutch or a cane?"

"We can try." Madison picked up the rod and set it on the bed before beginning her search. She managed to find a wooden clothing hanger in the closet and two potholders in the kitchenette. After ripping off a strip of fabric from the flat bed sheet, Madison brought everything over to Brianna and the pair set to work bending the metal hook of the hanger and wedging it into the hole on the end of the rod.

When it was tight enough not to wiggle, Brianna wrapped the pot holders around the hanger and wound the strip of sheet around and around the entire contraption until it resembled a single crutch. She held it out with a smile. "What do you think?"

"That I have an amazing best friend." Madison glanced down at her own injury. "I wish we had something for my hand."

Using the new crutch, Brianna managed to drag herself up to stand. She held her injured leg bent with her foot off the ground and leaned on the crutch. "This will work. Let's look for something for you."

"We don't have time. Besides, I can manage. Check the front door. I'll check the windows." Madison hurried over, but her hope soon faded. They were old, single-paned, and unable to open. She peered down into the dark. They had to be at least a full story off the ground. "We can't get out this way."

"The door is locked. It won't even budge." Brianna gave the handle a yank. "There's a plate covering the lock. Even if we had a crowbar, I don't think we could wedge it in far enough to pop it." She sighed and turned around. "I can't see anything through the peephole, either."

"Then we're trapped." Madison reached up and gingerly felt around the bruising on her temple. Her head still ached and every time she turned too quickly, it took a moment for her vision to catch up. Two of her fingers were mangled and she didn't know if she would ever be able to set them right again.

She slumped onto the bed, no longer caring about the grime. "We have no weapons and no way out. We're going to die here."

"Don't say that. We're not giving up. Not yet." Brianna hobbled away from the door and stopped at the foot of the bed. "There has to be another way." She crossed the room and threw open a cabinet. Using her crutch to keep her balance, she ran her fingers up and down the back wall.

"That isn't a magical wardrobe. We're not going to find a gateway to another world through it." Madison fell back onto the bed and a cloud of dust plumed into the air. The circle of light from the flashlight came to rest on a vent grate in the short wall above the closet.

Madison stared at it for a moment before peeling herself off the bed. She dragged a chair over to the closet and climbed on top. Using the flashlight, she inspected the screws and the space beyond the vent. "I think it's big enough. If we can get this grate open, we might be able to crawl out."

"How are we going to get up there?"

Madison hopped off the chair and opened the drawers in the kitchenette. She pulled out a beat-up butter knife and climbed back onto the chair. With the flashlight gripped between her teeth, she wedged the knife under the side of the vent and tried to pry it open. It wobbled, but didn't come free.

She spit out the flashlight long enough to talk. "Let me see if I can get it open."

"I'll search the rest of this dump for anything we can use."

While Brianna opened cabinets and drawers and looked under the bed, Madison managed to slide the knife blade into the screw top on the lower left of the vent grill. With painstaking effort, she twisted the screw until it popped free. "One down, one to go."

"I think we can stack these bedside tables. That should give us enough height." Brianna pushed the far table off the wall. "Ooooh! And I found a lighter!" She disappeared beneath the side of the bed and came back holding a glowing flame. "Plenty of butane, too."

Madison managed to unscrew the other side and used the knife to pop the bottom of the vent grill free. She shone the light down the shaft. "It's a return duct. Pretty big. Tons of dust and..." she groaned. "Dead cockroaches."

"I don't care if it's full of live rats if it gets us out of here." Brianna shoved the table again. "Help me move this over there and we can climb up."

Together, the young women worked to build a steady platform, stacking the bedside tables against the wall and using the bed to keep them stable. It wasn't the safest of climbing structures, but it would give them a means of getting up.

Madison climbed up onto the bed and held out her one good hand. "I'll stand here and help you up."

Brianna took ahold and grimaced against the pain as she stood on one leg. She looked up at the vent. "Here goes nothing." With Madison's hand gripping the underside of her thigh, Brianna used her upper body strength and Madison's leverage to make it onto the first table.

She stood up eased the crutch into the hole. "If we fall through the duct and into someone else's room, I hope they've got a bigger bed."

"Why?"

"So we land on it and not the floor." Brianna shoved her arms into the vent shaft and hooked her elbows over the opening. "Push as hard as you can on three. One, two, three."

Madison shoved her up, straddling the sinking mattress as Brianna scrabbled with all her might. After a few touch and go moments, her good leg kicked like a dolphin and she disappeared inside the shaft.

"When you said cockroaches, you meant it. These things are as big as chihuahuas."

"Can you see anything?"

The flashlight beam bounced around in the vent for a moment. "It ends in the T about twenty feet ahead. We'll have to make a choice which way to go."

"I vote for the path with the fewest bugs."

"Deal."

Madison climbed up the end tables and shimmied into the vent. The grate swung shut behind her and she low-crawled toward Brianna. "Let's find a way out of this place."

CHAPTER TWENTY-SIX
WALTER

Donner Lake
  6:00 a.m.

The lone sentry leaned back against a dented Toyota Tacoma, shotgun perched on his forearm.

"See anyone else?" Colt leaned close enough to Walter to whisper.

"No. But the way he keeps checking his watch, we've got to be near a shift change."

"Then let's wait him out."

"Tracy will be impatient."

Colt glanced behind him where the rest of their group sheltered in the trees. "Do we want to do this right or fast?"

Walter exhaled. "We'll wait."

It didn't take long. Within five minutes, another pickup truck rumbled down the single access road on that side of the lake and stopped beside the Tacoma. A man lumbered down from the cab, hair shorn close to the scalp, with a wiry beard stretching almost to his collarbone.

He hoisted a leather jacket over his expansive shoulders and plucked a hunting rifle off a rack mounted in front of the truck's rear window before walking around to shake the sentry's hand.

"All quiet?"

The sentry spit out a wad of tobacco juice and adjusted the dip in his lip. "Yup. Ain't seen nothin'."

"Good." The new man ran a hand through his beard. "Silas brought us back a couple of real nice presents."

"Yeah? Did he finally find that whiskey I wanted?"

"Naw, man. *Women.* Two real lookers. Young, too." He clapped the sentry on the back and the pair laughed and made a crude gesture that boiled Walter's blood.

They were alive. He tried to be thankful, but the urge to shoot the two men almost overwhelmed him. But as they assembled all the gear that morning before hitting the road, everyone agreed: no guns until they had no choice. They had to go in stealthily and quiet and deadly. Shooting would only alert the rest of the group to their presence and they couldn't fight off fifty guys at once.

After the two Cunningham men talked a bit more, the younger man on the night shift climbed up into his truck and started the engine. Colt motioned for two of their crew to follow him by keeping to the trees.

Walter and Colt waited for the right time. As soon as the bigger man turned back toward his truck, they took off, silent as their boots rolled across the asphalt. Walter's hand wrapped around the man's mouth from behind and Colt kicked him in the back of the knee. He fell and the rifle in his hands clattered to the pavement.

Colt picked it up. "We're going to ask you some questions. If you scream or try to alert your friends in any way, we'll kill you."

Walter pressed a wicked hunting knife with a five-inch blade up to the man's neck. "Is that clear?"

The man tried to nod, but the blade poked into his skin and he recoiled.

Walter let go of his mouth. "Where are the girls being kept?"

"I don't know what you're..."

Colt stepped forward and cracked the man's skull with the butt of the rifle hard enough to knock his brains about but not render him unconscious.

The man wobbled, but Walter gripped him tighter, bringing the knife back to his throat. "Try again."

"They're in the main building. A room on the second floor."

"Which one?"

"I don't know."

Walter pressed the blade of the knife deeper into the man's neck. Blood welled across the blade and dripped onto the man's hand. "Which one?"

"I. Don't. Know."

"How many of you are there?"

"Only Silas made it back after that ambush."

Walter was losing patience. He dug the knife in.

More blood spilled. "How many?"

The man whimpered. "Thirty. Maybe thirty-five."

"How many are a good shot?"

"Fifteen or twenty. The rest are girlfriends or kids."

Shit. It was more than he'd hoped. They would have a hell of a time taking them all out. Walter looked up at Colt. "That everything?"

"Pretty much." Colt pulled back and with all his might, slammed the rifle once more into the man's skull. This time, bones crunched.

Walter let go and the body slumped to the ground. He frisked him, pulling out another handgun, but nothing more.

Colt grabbed the man by the ankles and dragged him into the trees while the rest of their group emerged. "Everyone into the back of the truck. There are upward of thirty-five. Twenty shooters."

Tracy, Peyton, Anne, and Barry climbed into the back of the truck and Walter and Colt took the cab. As the doors shut, Walter glanced at Colt. "We're on the same page, right?"

"Kill first, no questions?"

"I'd like to spare the non-hostile women and all the kids."

"Agreed. What about the men who surrender?"

Walter thought it over. "Depends on the situation. But I'm not losing Madison to these thugs. They forfeited the right to a fair deal when they ambushed us and kidnapped my kid."

"Amen." Colt cranked the engine and turned the

truck around.

They headed straight toward the motel and as soon as the first building came into view, Larkin flagged them into the trees. They hid the truck twenty feet off the access road in a thicket of brambles and everyone piled out. Walter found Larkin near the road. "What do you see?"

"There's one main building with two floors, then a bunch of side buildings, outbuildings, and sheds that are all single story."

"The girls are in the main building on the second floor. No details as to where." Walter glanced past him to the Tacoma sitting quietly in the parking lot. "Did the sentry give you any trouble?"

"Didn't even know what hit him. Neither did the guy stumbling out to take a leak. Died with his dick in his hand, poor asshole."

Walter clapped Larkin on the back. "Good. That leaves upward of seventeen capable shooters, maybe that many unarmed women and kids."

"We going in hot?"

Colt joined the conversation. "These guys aren't early risers. We might be able to get in and out without blowing the place up."

Larkin checked his rifle. "Not a bad plan. This place is in a good spot. If we flushed them out…"

"I don't care if it's turned to ash. I just want Madison and Brianna out of here." Walter motioned to everyone to join them and the group huddled around, protected from sight thanks to the thick underbrush and trees.

"The girls are in the main building, second floor. Tracy and Barry, you'll take the east exterior door. Peyton and Anne, the west. Larkin and Dani will clear the first floor. Colt and I will clear the second. As soon as we find Madison and Brianna, we're coming out and we're getting the hell out of here."

"What if we get caught?" Anne glanced over at her husband. "Do we start shooting?"

Barry nodded. "We follow the plan. Shoot all hostiles. Leave the rest."

They talked logistics for a few minutes until everyone was sure of the plan before breaking off into pairs. Walter and Colt took the lead, running just inside the tree line toward the western exterior door. Unlike most motels, the rooms were interior facing with only windows facing the parking lot.

On the one hand, it meant they could search concealed from the outside, but on the other it made escape that much more difficult. On the count of three, Walter yanked open the door. All was quiet. Dani and Larkin eased past him and slipped into the darkness of the hall.

Walter took one last look at his wife and followed them inside. He had to stay strong, not just for Madison, but for Tracy, too. If they couldn't save their daughter, he had to ensure his wife made it out of there alive.

The dark enveloped him and he grimaced as the smell of stale cigarettes, old grease, and dirty socks hit his nose. Even after the apocalypse women and kids didn't live like this. The main building must have been the bachelor quarters.

He clamped his mouth shut and breathed through his nose as they eased down the hall. The only light filtering in came from the slim glass windows in the exterior doors. They illuminated just enough to be dangerous. It was too easy to miss a man pressed tight against the wall.

Fifteen steps inside, Walter spotted the sign for the stairs and motioned toward it.

Larkin nodded and took up position on the far side of the door with Dani guarding the hall. Colt opened the door. It squeaked on rusty hinges and Walter winced. Larkin and Dani might have the toughest job of all. He nodded at them both before slipping into the stairwell behind Colt.

He eased the door closed and Colt flicked on a tactical flashlight mounted to his Sig. He whispered as they climbed the stairs. "This is giving me the creeps."

"Same here. Shouldn't half this place be awake by now?"

"Maybe looting and pillaging and living by a lake has its advantages."

"Don't go getting any ideas. We need you to man the wheelbarrow in the spring."

The stairs ended at a landing littered in cigarette butts and empty beer cans. Colt sidestepped the mess and turned off his light. "I wouldn't dream of it. Now let's find your daughter and Brianna and get the hell out of here."

He counted to three and pulled open the door.

CHAPTER TWENTY-SEVEN

MADISON

Donner Lake
    8:00 a.m.

Madison turned and a spiderweb coated in dust enveloped her face. A mummified insect landed on her cheek. She bit back a scream and brushed the sticky fibers and decay away with her uninjured hand.

Even if they managed to rig up a hot shower somewhere, it would never fully wash the memory of the ventilation shaft from her mind. Tight spaces had never bothered her. She excelled at hide and seek as a kid, always finding the finest closet or space to hide inside, staying quiet and breathless under the bed while her mom tried to find her.

But a shaft barely big enough to slither through covered in fifty years of dirt and insects was too much, even for her. Sweat coated her face and dampened her shirt and turned the space inside her boots to rank puddles of stink.

At the first T of the shaft, Brianna had wiggled herself backward and waited for Madison to take the lead. Now she tapped her on the ankle and whispered. "I need a break."

Madison twisted, shoving her butt against the shaft wall and angling her head down enough to look at her best friend. The weak flashlight beam lit up Brianna's face covered in sweat and dirt. Her cheeks heaved from effort and dried tears tracked through the grime like abandoned creek beds in the winter.

Her injured leg and concussion weren't making this easy, but they had no choice. Madison's own hand screamed in pain every time she bumped it. Her head still ached from the blow to the temple.

"We can't stop. We have to find an empty room and get out of this thing."

Brianna nodded. "I just need to catch my breath. I never thought it would be so hot up here without the heat on."

"We're on the second floor. We've got all the heat rising from below and the sun beating down from above. It's probably the warmest place in the whole building."

"Remind me of that if we ever make it out of here. If we ever need to keep from freezing to death, we just need to crawl into a ventilation shaft."

"I'd rather freeze." Madison turned back around. "There's got to be a grate up here. Come on."

She shimmied through the dust, keeping the flashlight pinned to a small circle beside her face. It gave her just enough light to see a few feet ahead, but hopefully not enough to broadcast their existence.

Madison slowed as a junction in the shaft loomed. She eased up and clicked off the light before pulling herself into the split. A grate. Five feet down a sub-shaft, holes in a vent grate lit up with artificial light.

It could be their way out.

Madison twisted around. "There's a grate. I'm checking it out."

The shaft wasn't wide enough for both Madison and Brianna to fit, so Madison crawled toward the grate alone, sliding a knee and an elbow at a time, slowly enough to muffle any sound. As she neared the light, a voice cut through the dust.

"Christ, Kenny, that hurt."

Madison shied back. She didn't have to see the man to know who was speaking. It was Silas, the man she helped. The man who would have bled out if she hadn't used a tourniquet around his leg.

How did he thank her? By cracking her in the side of the head, breaking her fingers, and dragging her back to his camp like a caveman with a bounty. She steeled herself and eased forward, mindful of the need for stealth. If Silas heard her, he might shoot first and not bother to ask any questions.

As she neared the grate, the far side of the room came into view. Silas sat in a chair, legs spread out in front of him, a bottle of liquor propped on his good thigh. His wounded leg was exposed, blood oozing down his bare skin and dripping onto the carpet.

Madison forced a dusty swallow.

Another man she presumed to be Kenny stood beside Silas holding a red Solo cup and something metal in his hands. Madison squinted to try and see, wishing for binoculars or a scope.

"I can't get it out unless I find it." Kenny leaned over Silas's leg and jammed whatever he was holding into the bullet wound. Silas clutched the bottle so tight his knuckles flared white and he stared up at the ceiling in obvious pain.

His good leg thumped the ground.

Kenny scolded him. "Hold still, for God's sake."

"Just. Find. It." Silas gritted out the words behind clenched teeth.

Madison fought the urge to retch. She didn't see any medical equipment in the room. From what she could tell, Kenny was digging around in Silas's thigh with a pair of regular tweezers from someone's bathroom. The only disinfectant was the liquor bottle.

Kenny pulled back up with a grimace. "I can't get it. I keep hittin' your bone. It's got to be buried too deep."

Silas sucked in a trembling breath. His whole face paled and he struggled to bring the bottle to his lips. After drinking a swig he poured a shaky stream onto his bullet wound, groaning and stomping the ground with his good leg as the liquor poured over his thigh.

No wonder they wanted the pharmacy. Madison

leaned back. If he hadn't turned on her when he found out about the car accident, Madison would have helped him. She would have insisted that they use their supplies to clean the wound and find the bullet.

Even the limited knowledge of everyone at the Cliftons' place would have been better than this. She forced a wave of acid down her throat. It didn't have to go like this at all. But the longer it did, the better chance Madison and Brianna had of escape. She pulled back, ready to move on and find another grate, when a door slammed.

"About damn time."

"I should save these supplies and let you sit here, bleeding to death."

Madison eased forward. An older man stood beside Silas, holding a plastic shopping bag stuffed with boxes and bottles. His hair grayed at the temples and flowed down his back in wavy mats, and his beard touched his chest.

The gravel in his voice spoke of years of hard living and cigarettes, and the scar running across the back of his hand added to the image. He leaned over Silas with a face full of disgust. "You failed yesterday."

Silas shifted in his seat, physical pain temporarily displaced by the older man's words. "I came back alive. And I brought hostages. More than I can say for anyone else."

"You should have captured the drugs." He shook the bag. "Not just a few handouts."

Silas wiped at his mouth. "You should never have sent Nathan in your place. He started the whole damn mess."

"Don't you speak ill of your uncle."

"I'm speaking the truth." Silas leaned forward and held the bottle up for emphasis. "He shot one of theirs in the back. That's what started it. If he hadn't been such an idiot, we'd have taken them."

The older man backhanded Silas across the cheek. "Enough!"

Silas licked at a spot of blood pooling in the corner of his mouth and didn't say a word. The older man began to pace, stalking back and forth in front of Silas.

After a few moments, Kenny spoke up. "Did Silas tell you about the women?"

He turned and pinned Kenny with a stare. "He did. And we have plans for them."

Madison's blood turned cold. *Plans.* She knew what that meant. The older man must have been the leader the Cliftons had warned them about all those months ago. The elder Cunningham himself.

We have to get out of here. If he was that cold to Silas, what would he do to Madison and Brianna? Two members of the group who shot up his family. Two young women in a sea of men.

Panic filled her as horrible images paraded across her imagination. Dirty hands. Filthy sheets. No escape.

No one knew where they were. No one would be coming to save them. For all Madison knew, everyone else in her family was already dead. If she didn't get

Brianna out of that ventilation shaft and out of that motel, they would suffer a fate way worse than the scene playing out before her.

Her heart beat so loud she couldn't hear the men below and sweat broke across her palms. Madison backpedaled, hurrying down the shaft toward the junction and Brianna. As she tried to turn the corner, her sweater caught on an exposed screw. *No!* They couldn't waste any time. They had to go. *Now.*

She yanked her arm, desperately trying to free herself. It wouldn't budge. Madison pulled harder, jerking her arm up and down. The fabric ripped and her arm flew back. Her fist slammed into the top of the shaft. The metal warbled and the sound carried to the grate.

"What was that?"

"It sounded like the air duct."

"Check it out. Now!"

The men's voices carried and panic overcame her. Madison scrambled down the shaft. "We have to go now!"

Brianna struggled to keep up with Madison as she low-crawled down the shaft away from the men. Everything had gone so wrong. First the pharmacy, then the ambush, now this. They might never make it out of the motel alive.

She might never get to scoop up Fireball in her arms and nuzzle his soft fur or pet Lottie as she curled up on her lap. Hug her parents. Tend to the garden. Madison shoved it all down and increased her speed, forgetting all about the need to stay quiet. The shaft opened up into a four-way split and she slowed to catch her breath.

"Slow down! I can't keep up!" Brianna hurried to meet her, wincing with every drag of her injured leg.

"We can't!" Madison twisted around in a panic. She didn't know which way to go. She didn't know how to get out. To her right, another grate beckoned. She motioned toward it. "There! We can get out there!"

"We don't know who's in there. We need to scope it out."

"No time!" Madison hurried toward it and Brianna followed, reaching for her legs.

"Stop! Madison, no!" Brianna's fingers wrapped around Madison's calf, but Madison shook her friend off.

Visions of Silas all over her, pawing at her clothes and doing whatever he wanted filled her mind and she couldn't keep them at bay. She knew what they intended to do and she wasn't going to let that happen.

Those men wouldn't get her. She reached for the grate just as Brianna reached for her thigh. The other girl clambered on top of her, beating her with her fists. "Stop panicking!"

The metal buckled.

Madison turned. "Get off me!"

"Not until you stop!" Brianna crawled forward again. The weight of both of them in the shaft, scrunched in like sardines, was too much.

"Get back!"

"Stop fighting!"

Madison shifted and that was it. The metal gave,

screws stripped, and both girls screamed. They fell through the ductwork and insulation. Through drywall and paint and dust. It only took a handful of seconds, but it stretched on in Madison's mind forever. When her body hit the ground, she blacked out.

CHAPTER TWENTY-EIGHT

WALTER

Cunningham Compound
   9:00 a.m.

Four rooms down. At least ten to go. Walter motioned with two fingers to move forward and Colt nodded. So far, they hadn't found a single Cunningham. He was beginning to doubt the intelligence from the sentry back at the checkpoint. Had the man lied to protect his family? Were they on a wild goose chase while Madison and Brianna were being tortured in some outbuilding? Had they already died in a snowmobile crash?

He approached the next room and Colt tried the handle. It opened with ease. A wide shaft of morning light lit up an empty bed and dust-covered table. Another empty room. More wasted time.

The plan was all wrong. He stepped closer to Colt. "We should go back. I think this is a decoy."

"We should clear every room to be sure."

Walter opened his mouth to argue when a voice cut through the stillness. "Check it out. Now!"

Before Walter could even think to seek cover, a massive crash sounded down the hall. Doors flew open, banging against the wall and swinging back on their hinges. The place wasn't empty, after all.

Light from rooms with open windows lit up the hall in a zigzag, distorted by the hulking shadows of at least seven or eight men. Walter leaned close to the shadows, rifle tight against his shoulder, head down and ready. Colt sidestepped across the hall, mirroring Walter's position on the other side as a rush of bodies appeared.

Walter took aim on a skinny guy with his head on swivel. Two shots and he crumpled to the floor. Colt's work took out the next man, a real beefcake wearing nothing but a pair of boxer shorts and tube socks.

The two bodies clogged the floor, but the men kept coming.

A gun fired in Walter's direction and a bullet pierced the wallpaper above his head. They were sitting ducks in the open.

"Take cover!" Colt ducked back to the nearest cleared room and took up position from the corner, firing a series of shots before sneaking back behind the doorjamb.

Walter fired again before retreating, taking out a young guy of no more than twenty. "Madison!" He shouted above the din, hoping if his daughter could hear that she would know they were there to save her.

Colt volleyed another round of shots and another man fell to the ground. Walter leaned out and fired, straining to see through the haze and the bodies. Four down, three or four to go.

Colt shouted across the hall. "They're ducking into a room on my side." He tried to fire, but more shots rang out. Bullet holes pocked the wall outside Colt's door.

Walter called out. "How far?"

"Five rooms away."

Walter leaned forward and fired. A round hit a man's thigh as he ducked inside an open door. Walter hoped he hit the femoral.

That left at least two uninjured. Maybe more. He swapped out his magazine and sucked in a lungful of air before leaning out again. The hall was still.

He waited, breath hot and thick as he heaved. *Come on out. I know you're in there.* Walter stared at the light from the open doors. No shadows. No movement.

They couldn't have killed them all. What were they waiting for? He counted to three and took a chance, running across the hall to join Colt on the other side.

"There's at least two left."

Colt nodded. "They must be holed up in a room. What was that crash?'

"No idea." Walter wiped the sweat off his forehead. "But we need to keep moving."

A series of gunshots erupted from below them. Walter jerked. "Larkin and Dani."

Colt cursed. "There are too many of them. If they breach the stairs, it's over."

Walter refused to give up. "We can do this."

Colt patted at his chest pocket. "We can smoke them out."

"Do it." Walter watched as Colt pulled out two ping-pong balls covered in aluminum foil with an inch-long spout at the top. He used a lighter to heat the bottom of both until smoke began to pour from the openings, and then he launched them as far as possible down the hall.

They landed halfway between their position and the door where the men retreated. The smoke wafted through the hall, growing thicker by the second. When it obscured enough of the hallway for them to advance, Walter and Colt eased from the safety of the empty room.

As they closed the distance, voices grew louder and louder. One room away from the men, Walter and Colt took cover on opposite sides of the hall. The smoke was almost gone. Colt pulled out two more smoke bombs and repeated the process, this time throwing them into the open space in front of the occupied room.

"Come on, Elias. We've got to go. That's fire, man. Can't you smell it? We're all gonna get roasted alive."

"It's a trick."

"What if it's not?"

The men kept arguing and Walter was able to identify three distinct voices: Elias, the leader, and two other men. He didn't hear Madison or Brianna.

"Let's just take them and go."

"No. It's what they want."

"They won't shoot."

Like hell we won't. Walter checked his magazine. Plenty of rounds left.

"Then what?"

"We can worry about that later."

More gunfire erupted from downstairs and Walter steeled himself. He had to hope Tracy was holding her own outside and that Larkin and Dani were doing their job on the first floor.

As the ping-pong balls fizzled out, a man emerged from the room.

Walter readied to fire, but the man wasn't alone. Brianna stood in front of him, hopping on one leg. Blood tricked down her forehead and into her eye. Dust covered her clothes and hair. She looked like she'd been through a war. But she was alive and conscious, which was more than he could say about the last time he saw her.

The man held a handgun to her temple. "You shoot and I shoot her."

Walter cursed. He couldn't take the shot.

Another man emerged and his heart tripped. *Madison!* An older man held her by gunpoint and she staggered forward. She favored her right hand, cradling it as the man pressed the gun toward her temple.

Walter ached to protect her. His only daughter. Standing there hurt and afraid.

Colt held up a hand from his position in the opposite doorway, reminding Walter to stay calm.

The third man followed behind the other two, shielding himself with their bodies. He limped badly and Walter caught the sight of an open wound on this thigh.

Silas. Walter focused on him. Silas carried a shopping bag full to bursting and a handgun, but nothing else. He was doing his best to hide behind the other two, but it wouldn't work forever.

Colt leaned forward enough to scout out the situation before pulling back. He held up one finger and pointed first at himself and then the men.

Walter nodded. If anyone could take the shot, it would be him.

Walter held his breath as Colt took aim. He fired one round and pulled back.

Before Walter could check the accuracy, a door behind them slammed open. Shots careened into the wall. It wasn't friendly fire. He whipped around and fired three rounds while Colt kept his aim trained on the men holding Madison and Brianna.

Another door slammed from where they had entered and Walter's hopes sank. If the stairwell wasn't secure, that meant Larkin and Dani were compromised and his job just got a million times harder. Walter twisted around and braced his back against the wall. The girls still stood where he'd last seen them, but Silas lay crumpled on the ground.

He nodded his appreciation to Colt. It made sense to go after the loose cannon first. Now they had two hostages and two kidnappers to deal with. Not great, but not impossible. Colt lit his last smoke bomb and threw it behind them toward the stairs. It would give them a few minutes of cover.

"It's over!" the older man shouted. He tightened his

grip on Madison. "You try and shoot me and she's dead before I hit the ground!"

Madison struggled in the man's grip, breaking away enough to shout toward her father. "Take the shot!"

Walter glanced across the hall, but Colt made a slicing motion across his neck. *Too dangerous.* He wouldn't take it. Walter didn't know what to do. He couldn't stand there and watch them drag away his daughter. But he couldn't risk killing her, either.

Standing there, staring at his daughter, all he could think about was the first time she took a step. Barely a year old with chubby cheeks and dimpled knees, standing in the front yard, wobbling all about. She took one step, laughed, and fell down.

She was the most beautiful thing he'd ever seen.

And now she stood less than ten feet away and Walter couldn't close the distance. He only had one choice. He stepped out into the hallway and held his rifle over his head. "Don't take her. Take me."

"No! Dad!" Madison lashed out at the man holding her and Brianna did the same, twisting around on her one good leg before using the hurt one to knee the man in the crotch.

Gunshots rang out. One after another.

Walter couldn't tell the direction or who was firing, but his daughter was there in the middle. He launched forward. "No!"

The man holding Madison jerked, eyes wide as he looked down at his chest. Madison broke away and he fell, face-first, onto the hallway floor. Walter reached out, catching Madison as she stumbled.

Brianna landed hard on the ground beside him, the man holding her hostage falling a moment later at her feet.

More gunshots erupted at the other end of the hall and Walter spun around, clutching Madison tight to his chest. Larkin stood at the end of the hall, lit up by a shaft of light, a handgun pointed at a body on the ground.

Walter twisted back around as Colt emerged from the doorway. Both kidnappers were bleeding out on the floor. Walter sagged in relief. "Thank you."

Colt shook his head. "Don't thank me. I didn't take the shot."

"You didn't?" Walter looked up, confused, only to find his wife standing above the man who once held Madison by the throat.

Tracy fired a single bullet into the center of his skull. "The first one was for Madison. That one's for me." She kicked him once before lifting her head. Blood speckled her cheek and her clothes, and Walter couldn't love her more if he tried.

She wiped her cheek and smeared the splatter. "It's time to go."

CHAPTER TWENTY-NINE

TRACY

Cunningham Compound
    10:00 a.m.

Tracy reached for her daughter's hand and Madison rushed to her. "Thank God you're alive." She brushed her daughter's matted hair off her face and looked her in the eyes. "Did they hurt you?"

Madison held up her hand. "Pretty sure a couple of fingers are broken. And I've got a nasty bruise on my head. Whatever I did to my leg happened in the fall."

Tracy wanted more than anything to ask her about the details, but they didn't have time. She turned to Walter. "We spotted five more regrouping by the water. We need to get out of here before they catch us inside."

"What about Peyton and the Cliftons?"

"I left them just inside the doors and watching."

Colt lifted Brianna into his arms as Larkin and Dani hurried to join them.

Larkin gave everyone a quick nod. "We've taken out six downstairs. Based on the body count up here, we're looking at fewer than ten shooters left. Maybe only five."

Tracy spoke up. "There's a group of men assembling at the water."

"Any children?"

"One woman with a couple of kids sped off in a car, but that's it."

"Then we hit the men gathering outside and get out of here."

"Agreed." Tracy turned to Madison. "Can you walk?"

"With help."

Tracy hooked her arm around Madison's waist and helped her to the rear stairs. Walter led in the front, Tracy, Madison, Colt, and Brianna took up the middle, and Larkin and Dani guarded the rear. They piled into the first-floor hallway and looked around. No sign of anyone.

Tracy pulled out her gun and the rest of the party that could manage did the same. Colt set Brianna down and she leaned against the wall beside Madison. Walter and Larkin eased the door to the outside open.

A pile of bodies greeted them, followed by Peyton and Anne.

"It's clear."

As Tracy stepped out into the morning light, Barry

held up a handful of keys. "We've got our choice of getaway vehicles thanks to our friends here."

Tracy looked at the men now lying dead on the ground. All rough around the edges and worse for wear with threadbare jeans and thin jackets insufficient to fight off the winter chill. Complete opposites to the well-fed linebackers inside. "They must not have been part of the inner circle."

"Only a couple of shotguns between them. Easy pickings."

Larkin stepped forward. "I'll search the other buildings." Colt and Dani volunteered to go with him and the three took off.

Everyone else tucked themselves into a sheltered patio of the motel. It gave Tracy and Anne a chance to assess their daughter's injuries. Madison's fingers needed setting and her leg some ice, but most of her wounds were superficial. Brianna fared a bit worse, but nothing time and rest couldn't repair.

"How did you all get so dirty?" Dust clung to every inch of both girls and bits of drywall stuck to their hair and clothes.

Before they could answer, Larkin jogged back up. "All clear."

Tracy exhaled. "So that was the last of them?"

"The ones looking for a fight at least." Larkin motioned toward the lake. "Saw one guy run off that way. Pretty sure he'd pissed his pants."

"Should we chase him down?" Barry picked up a rifle. "We don't want to leave any loose ends."

"No." Walter shook his head. "As long as we make sure we aren't followed, we'll be fine. We ditch the cars, cut any associations with this place, and move on."

Tracy turned in a slow circle, taking it all in. The motel. The outbuildings. Picnic tables and a boat slip. In the summer, the place would be the perfect base camp for hunting and fishing. Combined with scavenging, a family could live there indefinitely without needing to farm. No wonder the Cunninghams managed to do so well.

"What about their supplies and weapons?" Brianna glanced around. "Shouldn't we check them out?"

"She's right." Larkin stepped toward Barry. "Give me the keys to a truck and I'll stay behind. We can load up as much as we can carry."

"I'll stay, too." Colt jogged up and nodded at Larkin. "We found a storehouse full of canned goods. We'd be stupid to leave it here."

Tracy disagreed. "What about the women and kids? I don't think we should take it."

Walter glanced at his wife. "Let's leave all the food but take the weapons."

"We were fortunate with our harvest this year." Barry echoed Walter's sentiments. "There's no reason we can't leave the food. But take all the guns. We don't need to give them the means to attack us later."

Colt and Larkin nodded and took off, meeting Dani halfway down the trail. Colt motioned that she would stay and the three of them disappeared behind the trees.

Tracy turned to Walter. "We should pack up and go. Madison and Brianna need medical attention."

"And Ben's been on his own a long time. We'll be lucky if he didn't try to crawl his way home by the time we get back."

Peyton shook his head. "Lottie's on guard, remember? She would never let him leave."

Tracy almost laughed as they all piled into two of the Cunningham trucks. They drove out of the motel parking lot, backtracking to where they stashed their own vehicles. It didn't take long to transfer over and hit the road.

By the time the sun hung high in the sky, Ben Jacobson's beat-up F-150 rumbled back into the Clifton compound followed by an old truck the Cliftons used. Tracy helped her daughter step out of the back seat while Barry lifted his daughter down from the other side.

They had made it. Tracy looked to the road. She wouldn't breathe easy until Colt, Larkin, and Dani were home, but the hard part was over. They rescued Madison and Brianna and the men who took them were dead.

So much had happened in the past forty-eight hours. They had gone from hopeful to worrying about the future with the Jacobson family to watching their new friends die and loved ones suffer.

But through it all, they had survived.

Walter stopped beside his wife. "Worried we've been followed?"

"No."

"Then what is it?"

She turned to him with a sad smile. "Is it wrong to be thankful they're dead?"

"The Cunninghams?" He slipped his arm around her and squeezed. "No. Our daughter is alive and safe. Brianna is back home. We couldn't save John or Craig, but Daniel might be alive. Ben is on the mend. Those are blessings. And we can be thankful for them every single day."

Tracy exhaled. Her husband was right. She could be thankful the Cunninghams would no longer pose a threat and sleep knowing they would be safe overnight. After staring down the road a moment longer, Tracy let her husband guide her into the cabin.

303 DAYS WITHOUT POWER

CHAPTER THIRTY
WALTER

Clifton Compound
 10:00 a.m.

Walter finished surveying the property with a pair of binoculars and pulled them down.

"See anything?"

"No. So far, so good."

Larkin nodded. "My guess is the people who were left will cut and run. No sense in staying when their leader is dead."

Walter agreed. "With the weapons you cleared out, they can't defend the place."

It had taken Larkin, Colt, and Dani all day to round up an entire truck full of guns and ammo. When they bounded into the Clifton place around eight the night before, everyone sat down for a hot meal and talked over the last few days. Even Ben Jacobson managed to take part. It had been a good end to a terrible ordeal.

Walter glanced toward the cabins. "Tracy is taking Ben home today. She thinks he's stable enough to move."

"Good. Heather and Jenni must be worried sick. I can't believe they haven't shown up here yet." Larkin stared at the road. "What does Ben say about the pharmacy haul?"

"After everything that went down, he's comfortable with us holding onto it for now. They're short-handed at his place. We can keep it safe."

Larkin ran a hand down his face. "It's been a rough few days."

"But we survived it."

"We sure did."

"The pharmacy is safe. We're secure here in the woods." Walter thought it over. "We can go back to being hermits and ignoring everyone."

"What about the radio? Any new transmissions?"

"I haven't listened."

"Aren't you worried about the Unified Military Force and whether they're coming?"

Walter shrugged. "When I first heard the broadcast, I actually thought it could be a good thing. It would get us on track to being a country again with supermarkets and police and schools. Money and jobs and all those things we used to spend our lives consumed by."

"But now?"

"After the last few days, I think I'm pretty damn happy right here."

"So what if the military shows up?"

"Let them have Truckee. We've got all we need right here."

Larkin let out a low chuckle clapped Walter on the back. "Sometimes you surprise even me, Walter." He smiled as he headed inside.

Walter watched Larkin disappear inside the cooking cabin. The more he thought about it, the more he knew he was right. They couldn't go back to the way America was before and he didn't want to.

No more worrying about what the neighbors thought or whether his boss would give him the time off to see his daughter's game. No more arguments with the homeowner's association over what color to paint their front door or whether his grass needed to be mowed.

All they had to do was focus on the basics: food, shelter, security. It was hard work, but every seed planted and every shingle repaired meant something. They were more than surviving out there in the middle of nowhere.

They were really living.

Walter swallowed the rising lump in his throat and turned toward the cabin where his wife and daughter worked on prepping lunch. Colt stepped down from the porch and waved, ready to take over the watch.

Walter nodded and headed over to the radio shed. He shut himself inside and turned on the controls.

He leaned over the microphone and flicked the switch. "Good morning. This is Walter Sloane, and today is the three hundred and third day since a solar storm knocked out power in the United States."

* * *

Thank you for reading book nine in the *After the EMP* series!

Looking for more *After the EMP*? You can find the rest of the series on Amazon.

If you haven't read *Darkness Falls*, the exclusive companion short story to the series, you can get it for free by subscribing to my newsletter:

www.harleytate.com/subscribe

If you were hundreds of miles from home when the world ended, how would you protect your family?

Walter started his day like any other by boarding a

commercial jet, ready to fly the first leg of his international journey. Halfway to Seattle, he witnesses the unthinkable: the total loss of power as far as he can see.

Hundreds of miles from home, he'll do whatever it takes to get back to his wife and teenage daughter. Landing the plane is only the beginning.

ACKNOWLEDGMENTS

Thank you for reading *Hope Survives*, book nine in the *After the EMP* saga. The Sloanes and their friends have been on quite the journey the past nine months. They've survived the end of the modern world and created a new one out of the remains.

I'm humbled that I've been able to share their journey with you and I appreciate all of your kind words and support throughout this series. It's been a labor of love. *Hope Survives* concludes the first season of *After the EMP*.

I'll be turning to my *Nuclear Survival* series for the rest of this year, so expect to see all of the characters from the prequel, *First Strike*, finally have their own stories!

As far as the future of the *After the EMP* world goes, I haven't ruled out a second season, so don't count the Sloanes out just yet.

Until next time, happy reading.
Harley

ABOUT HARLEY TATE

When the world as we know it falls apart, how far will you go to survive?

Harley Tate writes edge-of-your-seat post-apocalyptic fiction exploring what happens when ordinary people are faced with impossible choices.

Harley's first series, *After the EMP*, follows ordinary people attempting to survive in a world without power. When the nation's power grid is wrecked, it doesn't take long for society to fall apart. The end of life as we know it brings out the best and worst in all of us.

The apocalypse is only the beginning.

Contact Harley directly at:
www.harleytate.com
harley@harleytate.com

Printed in Great Britain
by Amazon

50600167R00147